TRISH DUGMORE was raised halfway up a mountain in North Wales and later spent much time in Scotland with her family developing a love of being out in the countryside, which has dominated her life ever since.

She has spent winters teaching skiing, summers delivering boats, arranging flowers in St James' Palace and The Guard's Chapel, cooking in chalets and shooting lodges, helping start a crab factory in the Outer Hebrides, farming in Devon and also running a bed and breakfast business. Alongside this, Trish, with a creative writing tutor, ran courses at her riverside home for budding authors.

One day she got someone else to do the cooking and joined the novel-writing course. *Larksong* is the result of this and has taken all the years between the foot-and-mouth epidemic to the COVID-19 pandemic to complete. Now it is finally ready for publication.

G000088349

Larksong

Trish Dugmore

SilverWood

Published in 2020 by SilverWood Books

SilverWood Books Ltd
14 Small Street, Bristol, BS1 1DE, United Kingdom
www.silverwoodbooks.co.uk

ISBN 978-1-78132-996-2 (paperback)

British Library Cataloguing in Publication Data
A CIP catalogue record for this book is
available from the British Library

Page design and typesetting by SilverWood Books

God gave to men all earth to love,
But since our hearts are small,
Ordained for each one spot should prove
Beloved over all.

Rudyard Kipling

Acknowledgements

Thank you for your relentless help, Tony, from across the ocean, and Penny, from across the fields. Much gratitude to Writer Ink for their endless encouragement over the many years of our monthly meetings and to SilverWood Books for their patience with my IT inadequacies and for their kindness.

Book One

1

The spring of 1919 had been a wet one in Devon. Old Tom Northwood was in the yard mending the door to one of the linhays. The wood at the bottom had rotted and he was nailing a horizontal plank across it. Not a proper job but it might do for another few months. He stooped wearily to drive in the last nail. The job finished, he rested for a moment, leaning against the wall and mopping his brow with a crumpled handkerchief. The lines on the old man's face were etched deep as though the endless passage of water along a riverbed had worn them further and further down. They looked comfortable there. He thought of his son, William, and how he had taught him always to carry a clean handkerchief and pocketknife, and he wondered if he still did. The news of William's Military Medal had come through at the same time as they had heard of Stan Tregoning's death. The village had grieved for another loss, but at the same time felt proud that the first medal for bravery in the Devonshire regiment had been in their parish. Pride in his boy had not eased Tom's loneliness and now, months after the end of the fighting the previous autumn, William was still not home. Spring sunshine glistened on the fine buds of the apple trees in the orchard. Tom was lost in thought.

The geese, grazing beneath the trees, suddenly gathered for their familiar charge. Necks stretched forward and wings working as if for take-off, they let out a tremendous cackle and headed for the orchard gate. An infallible early warning system – Tom knew that someone was coming up the farm track. Around the bend and into the yard came William, tall, handsome, but thinner. The dog knew him at once; there was no barking, just prancing all around him. A dance of joy.

"William…my boy…"

Tom held out his arms and for a moment the two men embraced. Once they had been the same height but now he felt smaller, or was it that William had grown? His precious son: the proximity, the smell of him, the joy mingled with tears came from deep within him and rose towards the surface. Drawing apart, suddenly shy at this upsurge of emotion, they regarded each other. Tom saw that the boy who had left the farm had returned a man, and William saw that the man he had left had become old. It was the spring of 1919. The waiting was over.

William, along with many of the sons of farmers in the Devonshires, had stayed behind in France to fill in a section of the trenches, covering over the blood, sweat and tears. The sun had shone down on them. They had stripped off their battledress and stooped bare-chested over their shovels, each man with his own thoughts. Each trying, but failing, to make sense of the past years. The repetitive action of covering over layer after layer of soil had helped them suppress the awful images, to bury them deep.

Now, William was home at Hawcoombe Farm and, far above, a lark sang in a blue sky. Both men were deeply moved by the other's appearance, but neither commented. Old Tom's ruddy complexion had been replaced by a strange yellowness, and his once-huge hands had become claw-like. But the same green-brown eyes gleamed with joy.

"Food or farm, lad?"

"Definitely farm. I've had a bite on the train."

"Better come and see the latest crop of calves then. First things first."

So often, William had walked behind that same old tweed jacket. Following now, he noticed that the stitching was no longer straining down the back seam. Instead, the cloth hung limply, and William observed with shock how much weight his father had lost and that he stooped. The first rumblings of concern stirred; above them the lark stopped singing. The sun disappeared behind a small cloud.

At the gate, they stopped.

"There, my boy, what do you think of that?" Tom's voice was full of pride.

William looked out across the field. For a moment he saw, not the glorious South Devon cows, but that distant group of cattle on the Belgian border. Fighting to stay in the present, he clasped the top bar of the gate. Stan, he did not want to see Stan. But like turning back the pages of a book, the explosion filled his mind. The image he dreaded came crowding before his eyes. He tried to gulp back the sobs. With eyes tightly closed, his body shook as if from a fever and he was unable to move.

An arm came around his shoulders, and far away he heard his father's voice, not his words, just the tone, as though Tom were comforting a sick animal. William had heard this so many times before and his body started to relax. This was how Tom had held William when as a small boy he had grazed his knee and the blood had run down into his sock and dried crisply. William opened his eyes and there beneath his feet he saw, not mud but green Devon grass. The cloud passed. Looking up, he saw the sunlight on the deep red of the cows' coats. He saw the dear familiar bulk of the animals, of Primrose and Beth, and their mothers and grandmothers. The lark began to sing again. The old man wisely made no comment and they moved on as though nothing had happened.

They went from field to field, easily slipping back into the old pattern, discussing the merits of each animal. William felt that his father was happier than he had ever seen him. Each detail of the breeding plan was passed from father to son. Five generations had been born in William's absence and there was much to say about why this bull had been put to that cow, and how the resultant bull calf seemed promising but had not yet proved himself. Why the Fillpale line had been allowed to die out, and how the Beths had surpassed all his greatest hopes.

Finally, the gate to the farthest field, Riversedge, was latched. They turned to walk home across the wide meadow, where to the south they could see Isambard Brunel's new railway bridge spanning the Tamar between Devon and Cornwall. The sun was setting, making the cattle glow in the evening light. They dropped down into the green lane sunk between the Devon hedges and, still deep in conversation, headed back towards the farmhouse.

Before they went inside, Tom said, "Want to see the horses, William?"

William knew how important they were to his father, so they crossed the yard and ducked their heads under the low doorway. There they paused. It was all just as he remembered it. He heard the noise of munching and smelled horse, hay, chaff and leather harness. But only two stalls were occupied.

"Where is Bess?" he asked in surprise. As he said it he realised that he should have said nothing, for his father stopped in his tracks.

"What happened, Father?"

"I had to shoot her."

"What! Why? She was your pride and joy. You loved that dear old horse."

Tom rested his arms on the top of the stall and slowly started to relate the story.

"You know that we all had to give up horses for the war effort. They gave us compensation, mind, but there was no arguing. Well, an officer and a sergeant came walking into the yard one day in November 1915. I had hoped they would have forgotten about us, tucked away as Hawcoombe is, right at the end of the peninsula. But oh no, here they were, bristling with efficiency. They asked to see the horses."

Tom closed his eyes for a moment and cleared his throat. He was remembering how it had been, the sun coming in low and how it showed up the dust and cobwebs as if they were seeing them through a haze, like a dream, sort of out of focus. The horses were tied by rope halters, each in their own stall, chomping lazily on hay from the racks, then swishing their tails and changing weight from one huge foot to the other, their shoes clanking on the rounded cobbles. Now he started to tell William the sad story.

"Well, there was Bess, her three-year-old filly Dobbin, and the two geldings. I better tell you just as it happened, William, although it breaks my heart. You never know, it might help.

"Dear old Bess was nearing retirement, but the man from the Min Ag said he wanted her. Well, you know she was my favourite, but head had to rule heart. I went to her side and explained that she was old and tired, not much work left in her. They took no notice, just scribbled in a little brown book. Then they had a good look at the other three. I wished I had not kept them in such good condition. They wanted the lot. They said they would come for them on the following Wednesday. They would pay us, but that isn't the point, is it?"

As Tom spoke, he moved to Dobbin's head and gently stroked that spot that was like warm velvet on the side of her nose as he had done so many times before. William saw the tears in his eyes and heard the anguish in his voice but on that November evening in 1915 Tom had been totally alone.

"There and then I decided to leave Bess for the moment and took Dobbin, as yet unshod, out into the darkening evening. As I passed the tack room, I grabbed the whip. We walked together to the green lane. There, I latched the gates at either end and freed the youngster. I cracked the whip and she galloped off in fear and panic. I kept her going – every time she came back to me, I sent her off at a gallop. The surface of the lane was covered in sharp stones. After a while she began to limp but I still kept her going – laying into her with the whip. After an hour of this

I led her back. Her head was drooping, she was covered in sweat and she was painfully lame. I felt desperate about the cruelty I had inflicted. I had to drag her across the cobbled yard and back into her stall. She had badly bruised soles, as you can imagine.

"I went back to the house and from the wall in the scullery got my twelve-bore, collected a handful of cartridges and returned to the stable. Now it was time to deal with Bess. She was not going to flounder in mud towing heavy gun carriages towards the front. She was not going to be ripped apart by shells and machine-gun fire. I knew what to do. I took her to the home paddock and I do not need to tell you the rest.

"Once that was done I just sat in the kitchen with that old grandfather clock ticking away and hoped that one day I would forget. But I haven't.

"On the Wednesday the young officer arrived first thing in the morning, fresh pink cheeks and hardly any stubble to shave; he came from a hunting family in East Devon. This was a terrible job he'd been given. Coming from that sort of background, I think he understood how I was feeling. He seemed to try hard to act as if he was just carrying out orders, tightening his Sam Browne belt to give himself more courage, sort of pulling himself together. Yes, he understood all right. He asked where Bess was, so I told him: 'She had terrible colic last night, kicking at her stomach – I walked her round and round the home paddock but she just sank down and tried to roll. Her pain was unbearable, so I had to shoot her in the field. Kennels came early this morning.'

"The officer knew. His own father had done the same with his favourite hunter. He understood all right. He turned away.

17

He watched Dobbin being led out – hauled across the lumpy cobbles. 'That one's no good,' he said. 'She's hopping lame. We don't want her, only the best.'

"As the two soldiers led the remaining pair of geldings away the officer turned to shake my hand. Within that hand-shake, officer and farmer, mine and his, there was a sort of warmth between us, an understanding."

As Tom related all this, he stood with his head down so that William could not see his face, not see the tears and the utter misery.

"So, she's dead. Poor old girl."

Tom turned and hid his face in Dobbin's side.

"I saved this one, but I could not save more than one. I let Bess down, I had let the country down and I had injured poor Dobbin. One of my worst days. But we still have Dobbin and her foal. I've called her Bess after her dear old grandmother."

"Sorry, Father." For a moment William let his hand cover the old man's as it rested on the top of the stall and then they walked quietly inside.

Sitting at the kitchen table, they both cradled strong, dark cups of tea in their hands. Tom knew that William did not want to talk about the war. He had heard that the other boys in the parish who had returned earlier had all been the same. They just locked the horror away; partly, they did not want to relive the awfulness and, partly, they wanted to protect those they loved from the reality and brutality of those war years.

"I heard that you had a tragedy right here in the village," William said, as talk of cattle eventually faded and an almost awkward silence lay between them.

"You mean the New Zealand soldiers?"

"Yes."

His father leaned back in his chair, which creaked. Once more he looked stricken with sadness.

"It was early autumn. I was just leading Dobbin down to the farrier to have her feet trimmed. As I was crossing the railway bridge, the express from Waterloo to Plymouth was approaching fast. I tried to get Dobbin into a trot so we'd be over the bridge before the train. We just managed it, but then it gave a short whistle followed by a longer one. I'd trouble keeping a hold of the horse, prancing about all over the road. Almost instantly, there was this sound. Like a great wet slap. The train's brakes shrieked. Dobbin was in a right old state. By the time she'd calmed down, the express had come to a standstill three hundred yards down the line. The slow train that had been heading upcountry stopped on the other track. Soldiers were shouting, screaming, doors slamming and there on the line were bodies. All mangled. I tied Dobbin up and went to see what I could do. Most of them were dead. Nine had been killed outright and one died later in Tavistock hospital. All lovely strong young men. Off to fight for their motherland. They'd just arrived that morning on a troopship in Plymouth from New Zealand and they died before they even reached their initial training on Salisbury Plain. You see, they'd had breakfast before they disembarked at about six in the morning. Hungry young chaps, they'd asked when their next meal would be. They were told that at the second stop the sergeant from each carriage was to jump down, go to the guard's van and draw rations. There was a lot of hanging about on the platform in

Plymouth and they were very hungry when eventually the slow train pulled out of the station. Following instructions, they all leapt out at the second stop onto the line but on the same side as they had boarded. They did not wait for the sergeant. They were ravenous, see. There was no platform on that side, so they were milling about on the actual tracks. The express came blinding round the corner and just mowed them down. I can't get it out of my head. The waste…and the poor parents in New Zealand. So far away. We're going to have a brass plaque in the church in memory of them, not that that will do much good."

For a while they spoke of Albert and how, just before he went up to the front, William had been told of his brother's death. He said, "I almost envied the poor sod. The conditions, Father. But I don't want to talk about it."

For the first time Tom admitted to his son how difficult he had found it to give the boys equal love and attention. This had made Albert's death even more difficult as he had also felt such guilt.

Both men bent over their cups of tea and drained them, quietly thinking and trying to shift the sadness of their thoughts and find a comfortable place to store them.

"I must to my bed, William. Good to have you home."

Tom rose from his seat and felt for the next chair top, using it as a prop as he slowly and stiffly walked towards the stairs. He seemed drained of energy.

Later, William went up to his old familiar bedroom. The iron bedstead, painted washstand and thin cotton print curtains were all just as he had left them. He lay in the darkness and realised that this was the first time for nearly five years that he had had a room to himself. He sighed with relief. He could hear no snoring, no cries of fear from the inside of a nightmare, no farts or belches, no swearing and no rumble of distant gunfire. Instead he allowed his limbs to stretch to the cool corners of his bed and thought only of his father. It was the calm that he felt when he heard his Devon burr, the inflection in it and the intimacy and comfort of it. No orders barkingly given, sharp and demanding, only the caress of advice gently given, always adhered to and stored away in his memory.

Beside his bed, on the chest of drawers, stood a candle and the tiny sepia and cream photograph of the mother he had never known. He had been her second child. She had contracted milk fever and died soon after his birth. All his love had been for the man he had just helped up to bed.

William's older brother, Albert, had joined up two years before the outbreak of war. It was in those two years that Tom and William had built an even stronger bond. There had been comfortable understanding between them. They had lived in great simplicity here on the farm, pleased to be free from the endless trouble Albert always seemed to cause. To William, Tom had never had to raise his voice, but Albert had been a different matter. He had a sharp face like his maternal grandfather. He was dark-eyed, small-boned and narrow-shouldered. Perhaps because of his dissimilarity to Tom's own side of the family, Tom felt a rejection right from the moment of his first son's birth. His endless mewling, and the way his young wife, Agnes, would stop anything she was doing to attend to his every need, irritated him. If he tried to hold him or soothe him, the baby would arch his back and howl even more loudly. From those early days a difficult relationship built up between the two of them. After William was born, with Agnes dead, Tom would sometimes find Albert leaning over William's cot, the tiny baby yelling in pain and the small boy laughing triumphantly. Tom would look for marks on the baby, but he would find nothing. But at bathtime later in the day, his attention was often drawn to red marks running down inside William's thick covering of nappies. Nothing could be proved, but they always looked to Tom like tiny pinch marks. He would also sometimes come upon Albert engrossed in the task of removing wings from flies. Tom harboured a growing, but hidden, dislike for his firstborn child.

William, in contrast, was one of those babies who was content, slept or fed or lay in his pram in the garden looking up at the leaves and gurgling happily. As soon as he could smile he would chortle and hold out chubby little arms to Tom, which, of course, made his father very happy and feel loved and needed. The ricochet went back and forward, reinforcing their relationship.

Once William was able to totter around on his fat little legs, Albert did make an effort to play with him, but his patience soon wore thin and he would laugh when the toddler stumbled and fell in the dust, leave him there and wander off. At other times they would go together to play on the swing, and William would be excited to be included by his big brother. But was it an accident that William would be standing waiting his turn and

Albert would push the wooden seat towards him with some force while William's attention was elsewhere? The corner of the seat would catch William on the side of the head and he would yelp with pain. Tom never saw these incidents because he employed girls from the village to look after the boys. They would change frequently and the boys did not really form attachments to any one of them in particular. Meanwhile, Tom's work on the farm took up all of his waking hours. When he returned home his eyes were only for William, and Albert put on a sulky face that only served to further alienate father from son.

While William was a stocky little chap who wanted to follow his father to every corner of the farm, his older brother hated everything to do with agriculture. Once Albert had started school in the village, Tom would take his youngest son with him wherever he went; teach him about the cattle, hold him high to scratch the base of their tails and laugh with him as a Beth or Primrose salivated with pleasure. At three years old William was helping with the lambing, two tiny hands delving into the ewe and pulling out the wet squirming creatures. Tom would squat in the straw watching and then the little boy would sit back on his father's knee while the ewe used her rasping tongue to clean the tiny bodies. The miracle would then happen and the lambs would turn into cuddly fluffy white babies suckling their mother, who was making guttural bleats of love to her newborn twins. Tom's pride in his youngest son blossomed. Meanwhile, Albert failed to thrive. His nose would permanently pour snot as he picked up every bug from the board school. He was thin and lacked energy; he would sneak off to his room in case he was asked to do any chores. When he heard his father's heavy footsteps on the oak floorboards, he would hide in the huge wardrobe that smelled of mothballs and stale clothes. At school, he became more introverted and, as an escape from the jibes of the other children, who sensed he was 'different', he buried his head in books. Even at break time he would hide behind the stone wall of the outside lavatories, reading quietly and hoping not to be discovered. One kind schoolmaster took him under his wing. He showed interest in him, asked him about his books and brought ones of his own into school for Albert to borrow. These were books full of adventure, armies and far-off lands. The young master was only a trainee and when he left to teach at another school, Albert's life seemed even more dismal than before. He craved affection but got none from his father, who was brusque and distant with him.

William was now taller and broader than Albert. He captained the games of cricket in the schoolyard and could hit the ball high over the perimeter walls, his teammates gasping with admiration. Getting home from school, he would run up the track to the farm. After rushing upstairs, he would change into his farming overalls and disappear to find his father. On the way, he would pause just long enough to tear a hunk of bread from the loaf on the dresser and stuff it into his mouth as he ran off to the fields.

Meanwhile, Albert would dawdle home, full of thoughts of far-off lands and adventures.

A few of the brightest boys in the school were put in for a scholarship to enter the private school, Plymouth College. Albert was one of three chosen to sit the exam. The other two were also farmers' sons. He told no one. He won the place and went home elated to share the news with his father. At last Tom might be proud of him. Tom's face did not change and he continued cleaning the horse's harness as Albert stuttered out his good news.

"I'm not sure about that, Albert. There will be expensive uniform, travel on the train, and you will pick up all sorts of posh rubbish that will be of no use to you back here. You're better off in Tavistock like all the other village children. I am glad you beat the Doidges' boy and Stan Tregoning though."

Suddenly, Albert was overwhelmed with defiance. He would go. Despite his father!

He turned on his heels, red with fury.

Next day, he went to the headmaster and pleaded with him to talk to Tom.

The headmaster looked into Albert's face and saw the anxiety, and the pain. He had heard from the young trainee teacher that he thought that Albert Northwood was an exceptional student. But he had been so put off by the boy's unfortunate manner, always skulking round corners, shirking any communal tasks, and unpopular with his peers, that he had not followed up on it. But he now thought Albert deserved a chance, and he agreed to make an appointment to see Mr Northwood. He sent a note home with Albert.

"Please see him, Father. It means a lot to me."

Tom was only really at ease out in the fields with his cattle or sheep or in the stables with his beloved horses. But he was now dressed in his Sunday best and in the parlour to await the schoolmaster. He pulled out his silver fob watch and noted that five minutes had passed since the appointed hour. He grunted with annoyance. Then he heard a knock on the front door.

Tom had never heard anybody praise Albert, yet here was this educated man telling him that his son was studious and hard-working. Tom liked to hear this and felt pride flushing through his veins. Maybe Albert had got something that might be of value in life. He was, after all, useless on the farm. He hated rain, mud, hard work, cold winters, hot summers, the smell of animals, and he got hay fever during the harvest.

In that moment, Tom made a decision. With Albert out of the way studying he and William could get on with the real work. He had seen the students from Plymouth College climbing off the train, always late at night and with satchels bulging with books. Perhaps it would be best. Grudgingly, he accepted the headmaster's advice. Albert could go to the posh school; he'd pay for the uniform, and the train fares, and the scholarship would cover everything else.

At the new school, despite his prowess in the classroom, Albert showed little aptitude for anything else. He struggled with sport of any kind, and quite quickly the other boys began to avoid him. He was always the one left with no partner to travel with or to play games with. If he had been teased in the village school for his bookishness, now he was teased for his rural accent and hobnailed boots. Progressing slowly up the school, he did at least develop a carapace and an ability to merge into the background.

By the time he had reached the top class, Albert had decided that he would join the army. In that way, he would get as far away as possible from Devonshire, perhaps have some

26

adventures and be part of a group, maybe this time accepted and valued. The Empire held many opportunities in far-off lands.

Two years later, war was declared. Albert had by then become a lance corporal. He had hoped to get a commission, but he discovered that you needed sponsors and to know the right people, whom he certainly did not, so he had entered the army as a private and had quickly been promoted, rising fast through the ranks.

William and Stan Tregoning from a neighbouring farm, two years older but a firm friend, had been gripped by the patriotic fervour that had swept the countryside in 1914. Tom had only protested a little when William, lying slightly about his age, had joined up.

"We'll be home for Christmas" was the cry. William had thought it was a glorious thing that he was doing, and his father had been proud of him, but he watched with a heavy heart as Stan and William, dressed in khaki, waved their hats from the train window, and slowly disappeared from view around the bend of the track.

Alone at the farm, Tom worked late into each night and rose early, but still could not get the work done. He employed two farm labourers but just as they were learning the ropes, conscription came in and once again Tom was on his own.

Tom heard little from William, whose letters were mostly questions about the cattle, and nothing from Albert. A stricken sister of one of the farm labourers came to the farm to collect her brother's possessions. Both he and the other worker had died on

1 July 1916 at the Battle of the Somme, along with 20,000 other soldiers. They had shared an attic room at Tom's farm but now they shared a grave in the French countryside.

Not long after this event, Tom saw the postman heading up the farm lane. It was not the time for the morning post so Tom knew what this might mean. A telegram. One of his boys. His legs seemed not to be a part of his body as he walked jerkily towards the door. The postman dropped the buff envelope into Tom's trembling hand.

"Morning, Mr Northwood," he said and, doffing his cap, he turned quickly away and hurried back down the lane, pedalling fast, knowing that this would probably be terrible news. Tom walked back to his seat by the stove and sank down into it. His heart raced and his mouth was dry as he ripped open the envelope.

42737 Sergeant A. Northwood has been reported
missing, presumed dead. Letter to follow. OC Steval

That was all. Tom could find little but guilt within him. The sad tragedy of the death of his unloved son – the relief that it was Albert not William brought another wave of guilt. He pushed the telegram into his waistcoat pocket, called the dog and walked out of the door towards the stables.

Tom did what he had always done. He buried his sadness and concentrated on his farm work.

Now, as he lay in the flickering candlelight, William felt ashamed. During the fighting, his thoughts had been about survival, about his comrades, about lice and trench foot, dysentery and shells. The work of three men for five years had fallen on his father. What had any of them achieved? He could have stayed home, a necessary part of the war effort, to help feed the country. What he had done was not glorious, and his father had suffered. The overwork, the loneliness and the worry had left a scar. In 1918, when the influenza epidemic had swept across Britain, Tom had eventually succumbed; although he made light of it in his letters, William wondered if it had permanently damaged his father's health. He could see that the cattle had become everything to Tom. To get them through in good condition for his son's return had been the aim that drove him. Now it was done. The fight was over. They had only touched briefly on Albert's death. Neither knew quite what to say.

That evening, with Tom sitting across from him beside the kitchen range, William could see that a great weariness engulfed his father now that he had returned. 'Farmers never make old bones' was a local saying, but his father was not such an old man. This was more than overwork, William thought. Next morning he would take his father to the doctor. That night William slept well. His war was over at last.

It had been usual for William's waking to be accompanied by the sounds of his father riddling the range, followed by the sound of the shovel scraping out the empty clinkers and ash. The swoosh of the coals being tipped into place would be the sign for William to jump up. But this morning there was a strange silence. Perhaps his father had slept in after the long farm walk around the stock. William dressed quickly in the clothes that had lain waiting for him in the chest of drawers for five years. A bit big. Down in the kitchen it was warm and the smell of stew lingered from the night before. The stove had not been riddled, a sign that his father must still be in bed. It was with mounting worry that William ran back upstairs and down the passage to his father's end of the house. It was too quiet. He knocked and lifted the heavy wooden latch. His father lay quite still, turned away from William towards the window. He walked quietly around the bed and with one glance at the bloodless face knew that all life had gone. Gently he closed his father's staring eyes and folded his arms across his chest as he had done for so many comrades during the years of fighting.

I never thanked him. Why didn't I thank him? thought William.

2

With Albert and his father both dead, the farm passed to William, who slipped back quickly into farming life. His father's clothes simply moved along the landing into his room, the black funeral suit with mothballs in the pockets nestled up against William's old battledress. Father and son were exactly the same size, or at least they had been until Tom's weight loss. If William grieved it was not evident, but it was a lonely life.

A new battle now faced William. He threw all his energy into the farm. He refurbished buildings and took great pleasure in making good the stone hedges that surrounded each field. Although his father had kept the herd in fine condition, it was at the expense of the general farm maintenance, and now a huge task lay ahead of William. Occasionally, the nightmares of his war returned. The images would reappear, especially of Stan's death. William was embarrassed at his periodic breakdowns. He told no one and raged at his own weakness. He absorbed himself in the routine of a farmer's life.

Socially, the highlight of each year was the one day in summer when every young man in the parish laid down his tools, put on his best clothes and headed for the Calstock Regatta. William set off with his farming friends and neighbours. A great gaggle of them left noisily from Bere Ferrers station. But William sat slightly apart. He found it difficult to just have fun. It was not part of his family tradition. The Northwoods were about work, not play. Crossing the Calstock stone viaduct between the counties of Devon and Cornwall made this day seem like a real adventure and there was an element of letting their hair down because they were away from their home base. William's mood slowly thawed, helped by the cider at The Tamar, the pub down on the quay, which was always their first port of call. Cornish cider was good and strong. The young men downed their drinks quickly, one after the other. The rowing races were only slightly observed; it was more an excuse for excessive drinking. Flash boats lined up on the north side of the viaduct. Four men rowed each craft, pulling a single long oar apiece using both hands. A cox sat in the stern. Muddy, polluted river water was whipped up by strong winds against the incoming tide. The young oarsmen would roll up the sleeves of their work shirts, or dispensed with them altogether. Their rarely exposed skin was white and vulnerable. Each team eyed the muscles of the others. A single-bore shotgun using live cartridges would fire into the air to start the race. There were cheers and oaths and a crashing of oars as the flash boats tipped one way and then the other. They swept under the pillars of the viaduct and on downstream. There were classes for young and old, which took all afternoon. Meanwhile, the boys from the surrounding area drank and lay spreadeagled in the sunshine. On the bank, picnickers sat on rugs enjoying themselves and children played. It was a rare opportunity to mix with young people outside of their parish.

At some point as the evening wore on, the young men's eyes would start to roam, keeping a watch for likely females. The girls, knowing that the time had come, would preen themselves, passing a hand over their hair to make sure it was drawn back, adjusting a bonnet, biting their lips to bring colour to them. They would walk with a sway of their hips and notice the men, who in turn would notice them and make a choice. William was very naive the first year, but after that there was always the same dark-haired girl who would at some point appear, drop into step beside him and, with very little preamble, guide him to the back of the scout hut. The cider blurred his vision of her but she was buxom and willing and led the way to a gasping, breathless coupling. Then there would be a dash to catch the last train.

"I saw you having a knee-trembler, you lucky bastard," Dave Doidge shouted from the far end of the carriage.

"Must have been somebody else," muttered William, puce with embarrassment.

It was the fourth year this had happened and at least by this time he knew her name; it was Ruby. Each time she sought him out more quickly and any pretence at interest in the rowing had gone. Now, they would go up into the woods behind the village; he would lay her out and quickly, with her eager help, expose her large plump pale breasts and wrestle off her bloomers.

It must have been 1924 when, a month after the regatta, William, busy hedge-trimming around Chapel Meadow, saw Ruby coming up the farm track. She was what his father would have called a brazen hussy, but she had served a purpose for William. Now, she was calling at the farm, and William did not like this.

"Hello, my handsome farmer."

William did not like the 'my'.

"I'm a bit busy, maid, what brings you out and about?"

"Day off, see. The pub is being refurbished or some such thing, building work being done, so they let us off for the day. Thought I'd come and see my favourite fella."

Again the 'my'.

She'd got fatter over the years; the broken veins in her face were perhaps from downing a few too many port and lemons at the bar in Calstock where her job was serving, and then cleaning up after closing time.

William felt repulsed, physically drawing away from her. He just wanted to get to the end of this line of hedge. He wanted neither to talk to her nor to touch her. He just wanted her to go.

"Sorry, maid. I am really busy. Got any other friends in the village?"

As he shuffled backwards a few steps, she realised her mission was in vain.

To save face, she quickly invented an aunt.

"Well, I better get on and visit Aunt Maud. She lives in Brook Cottages."

She turned and shouted over her shoulder, "Don't expect any favours next regatta."

She flounced off and William felt relief and freedom; he turned back to his hedge-trimming.

Most of the farms in this little parish between the Rivers Tamar and Tavy were tenanted. In 1921, the landlord had financial difficulties and sold off many of these holdings to pay his debts. Here, at least, William was fortunate, for his was one of the few farms in the area that was owner occupied. So, while his neighbours dug deep into their pockets to buy their farms, William prospered. He was also blessed with the weather, for his farm was free-draining and in the wet years that followed, his land did not become muddy and waterlogged. Instead, he grew fine grass, the cattle improved and the harvests were good. William, now well able to afford it, had the help of Walter Blamey, an old friend of his father's who had worked on and off at the farm for many years. He knew each inch of the land and loved it almost as much as William himself. Walter and his wife Edna lived in a small, damp, dark, rented tenement near the station, at the end of the village. The landlord had given them notice – the cottages were to be demolished and new ones were to be built, with inside lavatories. One day, Walter talked to William about this. He was worried and hated to uproot Edna, but he had to find somewhere else for them to live. That evening William thought hard and decided that it would be a good idea to do up the shepherd's cottage at the end of the farm lane, and to offer it to Walter and Edna. They could pay a nominal rent and the rest could be paid for in farm work, and Edna could help in the house. So began a very satisfactory arrangement. Now, with Walter's knowledge, the best horses were found to pull new machinery and these soon occupied a special place in William's heart, second, of course, to the beloved cattle.

"There will be no tractors at Hawcoombe while I am here, battering down the gateways and churning up the lanes." And so it was agreed between them.

Walter and William worked side by side. Sometimes they would talk but often a comfortable silence between them would last for long stretches of time. Building walls together, William would just be thinking and imagining the correct shape and thickness of the stone he would need next and there it would be, lifted to within his reach by Walter. He would grunt in appreciation and then, almost before the thought had sent a message to his hands, another wedge-shaped and perfect stone would be at his elbow. They both had a special love of mending these Devon stone hedges. From one end of the farm to the other, gates were rehung, stone hedges kept up and new linhays built for the increasing stock. But, without doubt, it was those stone hedges that gave both men the greatest satisfaction.

By 1926, an element of pride in his achievements had crept in. The hay was ready early that year and was the finest yet. There was more work than they could manage, so three extra boys from the village were enlisted to help out. Two local girls came to make the harvest tea and take it out to the exhausted men; one was Florence, Walter and Edna's niece, and the other, her best friend, Meg. As William showed the girls the spotless kitchen, his shyness with females was evident and the girls felt ill at ease. Normally bold and full of nonsense, Meg and Florence were silent in the warm, dark room. Unhooking the harvest kettle with the cork in the spout, William then led them to the dairy. Newly clotted cream lay ridged like a rough sea, cooling in great enamel bowls on the slate slabs. Edna had made mountains of scones. Strawberry and cherry jam from fruit grown in the valley stood ready in jars.

"Here is a ham and some cold beef. Could you carve them up into slices and bring them out too? Just follow the hedge along on the left of the stack yard. You'll find us all out there." Finally, William left the girls and hurried back to the field with the empty hay wagon pulled by two magnificent heavy horses: the grey, Dobbin and the bay, her daughter Bess.

Florence and Meg, liberated by William's absence, giggled about everything and nothing as they prepared the splits; in Devon this is what they called scones thickly spread with clotted cream and jam. They boiled the huge kettle on the range.

"He'd be a good catch, my dad says. Lovely farm and no landlord to pay," Meg said as she licked the strawberry jam off the end of the knife.

"Auntie Edna says he has funny turns since the war – something to do with Stan Tregoning's death." But as Florence said that, she felt she was being disloyal.

"Anyway," she continued, "he don't seem interested in girls. Push over that other bowl of cream."

The clock chimed six and the two girls hastily loaded the big baskets, making sure they were well balanced. Bonnets firmly tied, they went out into the sunshine.

Arriving at the hay field, they were greeted by shouts. At a word from William, the men threw down their hayforks and came over to the girls, while Walter went to the horses standing patiently in their shafts; he secured their nosebags and with their heads lowered, they munched contentedly.

Two old quilts deemed no longer fit for use and kept for the occasion were stretched out over the newly cut grass. The men lounged awkwardly, leaving a wide space around the girls and their baskets. William lay back, his hands folded behind his head, weary but happy with the way the harvest was going. Above him, a lark sang once more. The sound of easy chatter and the girls' laughter drifted further and further away. He dozed.

Florence studied him as he slept. He looked older than his twenty-nine years. There were already crow's feet around his eyes and sad lines leading down from the sides of his mouth. They made him look stern. In his thick, brown curly hair she could see more than a few flecks of grey. Even as he slept, worry seemed to haunt him. Not an easy man, she thought. A fly settled on his nose and she flicked the tea cloth above him to send it on its way. Waking with a start, William reached out for his rifle but found only the hayfork, and realised where he was.

He composed himself, self-conscious, aware of her scrutiny. He scrambled to his feet.

"Another load to the stack yard, lads."

At full stretch, the men forked the hay high up in the air, showing off in front of the girls. When all was finished, Meg and Florence clambered up on the wagon to sit on top of the load. They lay back on their hay mattress with bonnets askew, a glow on their cheeks and much giggling.

Many more loads had been brought into the stack yard by the time the sun disappeared below the Cornish horizon. After all the hired help had been paid and had wandered off down the lane, William took a lamp and went to check the horses. Inside the stable it was warm and quiet. Cobwebs hung down, heavily covered in dust; every corner was softened and festooned with them. The horses were eating their oats and their peaceful chewing, combined with the smell of hay and dung, eased the loneliness that he felt after all the laughter and good company of the hay harvest.

William had only just returned to his usual seat beside the range when there was a ferocious barking that alerted him to a timid knock at the door. Opening it, William saw Florence framed in the arched, granite doorway.

"Auntie Edna sent me for the empty dishes." She blushed, sending even more colour into her rosy cheeks.

"You'd better come in. Thank you for all your fine help today, maid."

William felt flustered as he turned back to the kitchen. He gestured to the armchair and went in search of the missing dishes. In the gloom of the dairy, he saw them. His hands trembled as he picked them up. He didn't realise that they were still wet from washing; they slipped through his fingers and fell onto the slate floor, breaking into many pieces. Cursing his clumsiness, he hurriedly collected the fragments and, in his haste, a sharp point of the broken china cut deeply into the soft skin of his inner arm. The blood spurted out. Hearing the commotion, Florence rushed in and quickly snatched up a cheesecloth to cover the wound. They edged back together to the lamplight in the kitchen, but by the time she had him sitting at the table, the cloth was saturated. Florence gathered up a towel and William came to his senses enough to raise his arm above his head, gripping the makeshift bandage tightly with his good hand. As Florence searched for the next binding she in doing so dislodged the oil lamp. It fell flaming to the floor with a crash.

Somewhere in William's brain, the combination of noise, darkness and the sticky warm smell of blood had him back on that hill in 1918. He started to moan and shake. He let his arm drop. Florence was quick-witted. In the faint candlelight that remained, she quickly dropped the old quilt over the flame and turned her attention to William. He was still shaking and sobbing. The towel had dropped from his arm and the blood was running straight from his wound onto the table. She rewrapped it tightly, held his arm up and shouted at William to stop. He seemed suddenly to realise where he was. With that came a great embarrassment. He stuttered out an apology. The flow of blood subsided to a trickle. As she tended the wound, Florence felt self-aware and a little afraid. She now understood what her aunt had told her. William did have funny turns.

Washing the blood off the table, Florence heard the clock chime ten.

"I must be off or Aunt Edna will be worried." She wrung out the rag in the sink. "Are you sure you will be all right? Just sit quiet for a while and don't be doing anything to put strain on that arm."

William half rose from his seat to see her out but she motioned him back.

"I'm so sorry." He sank down. "Don't tell anybody."

"It's our secret," she whispered and was gone.

Next morning, apart from a throbbing in his arm, William was well enough for work but followed Florence's advice and avoided lifting anything heavy. The real damage was to his confidence. As he saw these outbreaks as weakness, William thought the best way to avoid them was to absorb himself in work and routine. He put all his energy into the farm.

3

Walter was suffering from arthritis. Years of cold and hard work had worn him out and in the winter his bronchitis meant he was bedridden. William worked on alone. He had seen one of the newfangled tractors being demonstrated at the local show. He did not feel tempted. It was very expensive, noisy and he wondered if it would even get through some of the gateways at Hawcoombe Farm. As he fed the horses that night he reassured them in his quiet voice and gently stroked the soft-as-velvet sides of their big faces and breathed in their special smell.

Between the wars William plodded on, putting one foot in front of the other. He did not acknowledge his loneliness or the passing of the years; he just kept going.

Sitting beside the stove in the farm kitchen one evening, William now read in the paper about the events in Germany, of the rallies and the pugnacity of their leader, Hitler. There was a time of uneasy peace and then war was declared and once more, so soon, the countryside rallied to the call and emptied of young men. William was left farming alone, struggling to keep up with the work. The fear that England would be starved out, that no imports would get across the ocean, was very real. The British must be able to feed themselves and every farm must produce as much food as possible. The Ministry of Agriculture was pressing William to plough up more land and plant potatoes in every possible corner. He hated the interference and felt infuriated that he should be made to destroy acres of perfect permanent pasture. Then the Ministry sent him two land girls.

A fine drizzle had started to fall and William pulled the clothes roughly off the line, making the wooden pegs fly across the yard. He heard the church clock strike the hour and knew he must hurry to the station to collect the girls. Really he was shy and could not imagine what it would be like to share his farmhouse with two strangers – and females at that. But his diffidence presented itself as bad temper. He threw the damp clothes into the basket and shoved it under the lean-to. The door of the van shed a fine spray of rust as he slammed it behind him and crashed the gears in his haste to be on time for the train. As he drew up he saw what must be his girls standing together, fighting to get their scarves tied over their quickly dampening hair. One was tall and handsome, the other small and neat. They were dressed identically in land girl uniform, green Burberrys covering over cord britches with heavy brown leather shoes.

"Over here if you are bound for Hawcoombe," he shouted and both girls ran across to him, dodging the puddles. He tipped the front seat forward to let them into the back and in doing so realised that he had not cleaned it out since he had shifted the ram. There was a pungent smell of sheep and lingering testosterone. He turned to greet them, his face scarlet with embarrassment.

"I am William Northwood and let me see if I can get your

names right. You must be Nancy and you must be Elsie. Am I right?" It was a guess.

He bundled their many pieces of luggage into the van through the back doors. How could they ever need so much?

"Yes, you are right, I am Nancy and this is Elsie." The taller one giggled as, showing far too much leg, she squeezed into the back seat. Elsie struggled in behind her and William glanced in the rear-view mirror to see a look of horror pass between them as the overwhelming sheep smell of the interior engulfed them.

"Oh my, Mr Northwood, what have you had in here? It's a revolting stink."

"You can call me William, and that is just the ram I moved down the lane. His job is done, see. I'll not be needing him until next mating season. Either of you done any farm work?" he asked hopefully.

"I once helped a cousin in Cheshire with haymaking."

This was in a shrill voice with a strong Liverpool accent. Must be Elsie, thought William. He glanced in his mirror; the big handsome one, Nancy, was busy applying lipstick.

"Can't say I have. But I do love animals. We only had a cat though."

William sighed. It was going to be as bad as he'd imagined. Back in the yard Elsie eyed the farmhouse and said, "Oh my, it's ever so old, like an ancient painting."

"It does us fine," William said defensively.

During the following week the girls settled and each morning went off to the potato fields to lift the crop and load them in sacks onto the trailer.

Their manicured hands soon became calloused but their

complexions improved in the autumn sunshine. At first there was much complaining about their sore backs. On their only day off William showed them where the pub was and hoped they would behave well as he felt it was a reflection upon him.

Now, a week after their arrival, William was settled at the kitchen table with his paperwork arrayed around him. He knew by the sound of her high heels clattering down the wooden stairs that Nancy was approaching and determinedly he kept his head down, crouching closer over his ledger. He felt her warm presence near him and smelled the unfamiliar perfume around her.

"I'm off now."

His good manners forced him to raise his head. Out of her uniform, she was as joyful as a bird escaped from a cage. None of the lumpiness of the baggy breeches and the green regulation jersey, several sizes too big, remained. Instead, wearing a well-fitted steel-grey blouse, she looked sleek as a seal. The buttons strained over her comely figure. William dragged his eyes away, but no detail had escaped him. A belt of matching leather was tightly fastened around a surprisingly small waist. William's eyes quickly moved upwards, embarrassed by his own interest. Already, after only one week in the fields, she had caught the sun and her peachy skin had a ripe glow. Then there was that mane of hair – thick, chestnut and gleaming in the light of the fire. It was exactly the same colour as the coats of the cattle. He felt a strange sense of familiarity.

None of William's observations were discernible to Nancy, who, in front of him, felt plain and unappreciated. She was used to turning men's heads, after all. Her high spirits drooped, but she was also determined to keep her true feelings secret. She swirled around. As she did so, William quietly eyed the neat ankles and the slightly rounded calves.

"Don't know when I'll be back. It depends."

"As long as you're down here by 6am for milking, it's no odds to me." William's eyes returned to the pile of Ministry of Agriculture forms. The door slammed shut, and a gust of wind fluttered the papers onto the floor. William felt disturbed.

Nancy caught up with Elsie at the gate. Elsie's appearance had not changed. She'd painted her lips, but was so proud of her new uniform that she had decided to keep it on. They looked as though they were off to two quite different parties.

The moon was high and full and gave enough light for them to find their way down the farm track to the village hall.

"Miserable old bugger."

Nancy hitched up her skirt and pulled her blouse down tighter over her chest.

Elsie giggled.

"Mind out, someone'll see you," she said.

"I don't care. All the people round here think about are cows and food. Our only hopes are those Yanks over the hill. They might even be there tonight."

"I think William's a good-looking bloke, and he's got ever such nice manners," Elsie said, as she ran a hand over her permed peroxide curls.

"You always get every man you want, Nancy. Bet you could have him if you tried."

Nancy felt a frisson of excitement.

Elsie continued, "Within two months I reckon I can get a pair of nylons out of the Yanks and you can bed our surly farmer. In fact I'll make a bet with you, Nancy. The one who wins gets first go in that dreadful tin bath for the rest of the year."

It must have been six weeks later when the night raids on Plymouth started. Elsie and Nancy sometimes crept out, closing the blackout curtain behind them. They would go to the highest point on the farm, near the rabbit warren, and watch the red glow grow bigger around the dockyard. The dotted lines from the anti-aircraft fire mingled with the shafts of bright searchlights criss-crossing the sky. The scene of devastation brought a feeling of excitement.

"Poor sods," said Elsie quietly. They never saw William on their late-night excursions. One night, as they had crept downstairs on their way out, they had heard a whimpering noise from his room.

"Must be the dog," whispered Elsie. The collie, Tig, slept on a rug beside William. This was surprising as working dogs were almost invariably kept out in kennels in all weathers. But Tig never left her master's side. Even when William shut himself in the privy down the garden path Tig would lie looking sad and abandoned just a foot from the door. When William reappeared, she would greet him with wild enthusiasm as if they had been lost to each other for hours. At mealtimes, Tig would lie under his chair. In front of the girls, William would only grunt at the dog and chastise her for the slightest misdemeanour. But Nancy had noticed that, when he thought himself alone, his hand would rest on Tig's head and he fondled her ears. He spoke endlessly to her. Nancy could not hear the words, but the tone was gentle and loving. Now, the girls stood very still. Nancy heard the whimpering again. Elsie pulled at her sleeve impatiently and they tiptoed out into the darkness.

William lay on his iron bedstead; the flickering flame of a single candle dimly lit the room. He was cold and he gathered the blankets and eiderdown close around him to stop the draughts. In the semi-darkness, he listened to the little owl perched outside on the pine tree. It was a sound that had haunted him with unimagined sadness and longing twenty-four years earlier.

He was never sure what had made that same noise out there in no-man's-land.

Could it have been an owl? Surely not. No living creature could ever have chosen to be in that dreadful landscape of dead tree stumps, craters full of mud and corpses, spent cartridge boxes and twisted wire.

Now, as he lay curled up against the cold, William tried to blot out the vision. He was, after all, in the place that he had longed for. He was home at Hawcoombe. But the cries of the men came out of the night, the noise of the shells falling so near. He put his hands over his ears, but the sounds seemed to be trapped within him and became louder. Now, he was on Hill Sixty with the Machine Gun Corps. He felt the comfort of having his dear childhood friend, Stan, beside him. There were four of them on that hill. Behind and around them was a stand of beech trees and some, despite the bombardment, still held on to their leaves. The Vickers gun was well positioned and padded with sandbags. They had done a good job. The four were all farmers' sons from West Devon. The familiar sound of the others' voices gave each of them comfort. William had paused to catch his breath and he looked around him. To every side there was grey mud; his mind drifted away from this moon landscape and thought of home. The squelch of his boot coming out of the ground suddenly awakened some distant memory of Devonshire fields in winter and, just for a moment, he succeeded in blotting out the present, and his mind drifted. Far away to the right, he could see a green field, like the Promised Land, and he could just make out the cows. Not the right colour, of course, not the reddy-brown of his South Devons, but he felt his heart contract with longing for the fields so green and lush, divided by lovingly tended stone hedges.

"Come on, you idle bugger. Stop daydreaming," shouted Stan good-naturedly, turning to face him. The two men from Ivybridge were reloading. Galvanised into action, William moved forward. As he did so, a sniper's bullet smashed into the back of Stan's head. His face exploded as he fell forward onto William, who was sprayed with blood and brains. It was not sorrow but anger that devoured William. There was nothing to be done for his dear friend but to avenge his death. Fury against the enemy, the army, the war and God overwhelmed him. The rage became a desire to kill. The other two men were cowering below the sandbags, well out of any sniper's vision.

"Get up and help. Reload!" he shouted. A shell landed very close. The explosion seemed to be inside William's head. Leaping down, he grabbed the handles on either side of the gun and fired the entire magazine of bullets, watching them rip along the top of the German trench. His aim was steady and relentless. Turning impatiently for the reloading, he saw that the same sniper had continued with his deadly aim. He had got both the Ivybridge men. Both shot in the head. Once more he knew that they were definitely dead. More anger swept through him. He kept low and reloaded, an overwhelming heavy job alone, but adrenaline fuelled his fury as he scrambled back into the firing position. For five hours he did the work of four men. Later, he could never recall those missing hours. It was dark when firm hands prised him away from the sights of the Vickers gun. The Corps were being moved back. He remembered seeing his gas mask rolling away from him down the steep side of a shell hole. He had not cared.

4

Meanwhile, as William lay reliving his terrors, the girls had walked out to Riversedge. The nights were long and colder now and both girls had pulled on their overcoats. There was no moon, and the ground was getting muddier daily. They walked close to the edge of the lane, where some clods of earth were still green. Across the fields, the glow of Plymouth lit their way. Tonight, the sky was aflame. A brisk south-easterly wind brought the smell of burning wood; flakes of ash drifted up towards them. They stood with arms around each other's shoulders and thought private thoughts. Elsie was thinking of her brother out there on the cold sea in the northern convoys. Nancy was thinking of the Americans just upriver manning the gun emplacements at Higher Birch. She imagined them with their easy charm, chewing gum, cracking jokes and waiting. She thought of Charlie. She remembered his creeping hands in the village hall as they danced to Glenn Miller and how her body had wanted to press nearer and nearer to his. Then there had been an air raid on Plymouth and the boys had left in a hurry, their open jeeps roaring into action as they swept off back to Higher Birch, leaving only the smell of petrol behind them.

The cold wind now persuaded the girls to retrace their steps. Back at the farm, pushing open the heavy door, they ducked under the blackout curtain. Nancy tiptoed towards the larder; she was always hungry with all the physical labour. Elsie signalled that she was going on up to bed. Quietly, Nancy opened the cupboard door and as she did so she heard two separate sounds through the low plaster ceiling. One was definitely Tig, but the other, she was sure, was muffled weeping, a sound so despairing. She made a quick decision, forgot her hunger and crept up the stairs. Instead of turning left at the top, she turned right towards William's end of the house. She gently lifted the latch. His room was lit by one candle. On the iron bedstead, under an eiderdown, she could see William. He was lying face down with his hands over his ears. She could see he was shaking and sobbing. The dog, in her distress for her master's pain, had put two forbidden paws on the bed, and was pressing her head towards him. Nancy's reaction was primitive and instant. Standing beside the bed, she gently stroked the hunched back under the eiderdown. Slowly, the rigid tension lessened. The shaking slowed until it became spasmodic. The breathing became more even. In the candlelight, Nancy felt herself calmed. She sat on the edge of the bed, the tiredness catching up with her now that the sobbing had ceased. She kicked off her shoes and lifted her legs onto the bed. William turned towards her and she nudged him and made room for herself, lifting the blankets so she could get in next to him. She leaned across and blew out the candle flame. Tig returned to her rug on the floor.

*

As the morning light filtered through the thin curtains, so William slowly surfaced, and with that came the realisation of what had happened the night before. No Nancy in his bed now, but the blankets were in turmoil and the unaccustomed smell of her perfume on the sheets brought it all back to him. Even alone, he blushed and closed his eyes tightly. Now what? He had felt awkward enough with the girls before this had happened. How should he behave? He felt, of course, a physical sense of languid relief, but the guilt was quickly moving in to smother it. From the light through the curtains, he could tell it was time to be up and milking. He wanted to be downstairs, and preferably out, before the girls appeared.

By the time Nancy and Elsie were up, William was already in the milking shed. He was tipped forward on his stool with his head resting on Beth's side, the comforting smell of cow in his nostrils, and in his ears the sound of the fine strong stream hitting the side of the bucket. As the pail filled, the tone lowered and bubbles formed on the top of the creamy milk. William felt calmer.

A shadow stole across the parlour. They had arrived.

"Morning, William," they said in unison.

"Morning."

"What task of torture for us today?" This from Elsie.

Looking sideways at them, William could see Nancy's silhouette in the doorway. The pale-brown regulation dungarees and green Aertex shirt did very little to disguise her figure and William remembered how it had felt as he had run his hands over her. Colour rose in his cheeks and he turned his head away along Beth's flank.

"Elsie, check the stock in Lodge and Archmoor. Look out for maggots in the ewes. Check each cow's udder. Make sure the calves are all sucking. Nancy, get the dung cart and shift some of that midden. Use Blossom. Her harness is the one on the left-hand hook. Walter'll be here shortly. Go out to Riversedge with him and unload. Start the heaps along the north hedge. Walter will keep you right."

This was the longest speech that either of them was going to hear that day. Even the brazen Nancy seemed to have the wind taken out of her sails. He had been dismissive and had given her the worst job. Fury replaced Nancy's good humour, and a determination crept in. She'd get her own way.

The scene was set for what was to follow. William could not bear to be near the girls. In the mornings, he'd give them their jobs, choosing always a task for himself as far away as possible. Nancy tried flirting but got no response. Walter's wife, Edna, now came to cook for them all at the farm. William would eat first, timing his arrival in the kitchen before theirs. The few words with Edna were a relief for him.

It was the endless proximity of the girls that frightened him. He didn't want to share his bed or his life. He felt on edge with Nancy around. He felt judged. He'd been used to a peaceful coexistence with his father and the enforced comradeship in the trenches. He longed to have the place to himself with no one to hear or see his shameful shaking and sobbing, and anyway, on his own, it rarely happened nowadays. When Nancy realised that she was being rejected, she stopped demeaning herself and a frozen awkwardness came between them. The only good thing was that she had won the bet and always had first turn in the tin bath.

*

Week followed week and ploughing began, a slow job walking behind the horses. Sometimes, William would almost fall asleep, waking only when the plough jumped out of the furrow. One day, Nancy brought out his lunch.

"Thanks, put it down by the hedge. I'll have it later."

She wasn't going to be put off.

"I've something to tell you, William."

She walked alongside him, the horses' harness jingling while all around them, the gulls shrieked and dived for the worms under the newly turned earth. Nancy's work boots caked with mud as she struggled from furrow to furrow.

"If you won't stop, then, I'll tell you now. I'm going to have a baby." William carried on walking. There was no outward sign of the total panic rising within him.

"Did you hear me?" she shouted. "What are we going to do?"

"I'll think about it, and when I get back after work, I'll tell you." So she was forced to turn home, lifting her legs high over the furrowed earth and dropping the lunch bag at the foot of the hedge on her way.

William came from a very respectable family and he was a man of honour. There was only one thing he could do. He worked out the dates as he had so often for his cows. He'd have to marry her, and quickly too.

It fell on Edna's shoulders to make all the arrangements for the wedding. It was rather a sombre affair. After the formalities in the registry office in Tavistock, only a few neighbours and cousins came back to the farm for a small reception. Elsie came from Portsmouth for the day, her hair tightly permed and an engagement ring on her finger. She had left the farm a few weeks earlier for a job in the Portsmouth dockyard and a chance to be near her Navy boyfriend, and her brother. Both of them had been posted there after months at sea on the northern convoys.

It was instantly obvious to Nancy that William was going to allow no changes at the farmhouse. The water had always been pumped in the yard, and he saw no reason to alter that. The village might have got electricity but they were fine as they were. Nancy's excitement at being married wore off quickly.

They did share a bed in William's room, but he hated the fripperies she brought with her, so all these, along with the bottles of hair colour, scent and lotions, were kept in Nancy's old room.

Edna continued to clean and cook but Nancy, as William's wife, was expected to take any spare farm produce to the market in the pony and trap. Nancy liked the idea of this as she could dress up a little and show off. But first she had to catch Polly the pony and learn to put on her harness. This was not easy and Polly played her up and at the sight of her galloped off, shaking her head. William would hear the drumming hooves and saunter over to the little pony and drape an arm around her neck, bring her in and show Nancy once more how to tack her up. Then together they would load butter, eggs and any other produce, sometimes even live chickens, into the little cart.

"Next time you'll have to manage on your own. I am too busy for this." William stomped off.

Eventually Polly and Nancy got used to each other and came to an understanding. This was not echoed by her relationship with her husband. He seemed to withdraw from her and within weeks, Nancy became bored. She was used to the constant bustle of people around her. She flicked restlessly through some old magazines Elsie had left behind. She was young, she knew she was pretty, but William made her feel old and plain. Each night he would sit bent over his bookwork, hardly noticing if she were there or not. She missed Elsie's company and started going to the pub on her own. The Americans were still manning the anti-aircraft guns at Higher Birch. They came down to the pub when their shifts allowed. Nancy's friendship with Charlie grew. With his easy ways and generous supplies of Lucky Jim cigarettes, he was so different from William.

Nancy's trim figure did not seem to change. William, studying her as he would one of his cows, became anxious and encouraged her to eat more. Smelling cigarette smoke on her clothes, he remonstrated with her.

"It's not right you know, you off at the pub."

"Well, you're no company sitting here with your bookwork. What's a girl meant to do?"

"Smoke's bad for the baby too."

Nancy lied, saying that it was only the smoky atmosphere in the pub and that she never touched a cigarette herself. However, she stayed out later and later.

5

One evening, William finally closed his books at midnight. That day Edna had talked to him while he drank his mid-morning cup of tea. Gently, she had warned him that there was gossip in the village. Some said that Nancy could not be pregnant and keep that fine figure. Maybe they were jealous. Others said she was getting far too friendly with the Yanks and one in particular. William felt humiliated, hating being the subject of village tittle-tattle, but he kept his anger well below the surface.

Later that same day, William had returned from the evening milking to find that Nancy had left for the village, the smell of her heavy scent still hanging in the air. So William had worked on. Now, it was late and the pub had long since shut its doors. So where could she be? He sat beside the stove and waited. Anger kept him from dozing off. Finally, he got up, opened the door and carefully replaced the blackout curtain behind him. He stepped out into the darkness and listened. Far away, he could hear the rata-tata-tat of anti-aircraft fire, and he pitied the poor people of Plymouth. The clouds were rushing across the sky. On the other side of the yard, the barn was at one moment glowing in the moonlight and then plunging back into darkness.

Looking back later, William was never sure what he had seen that night. Was it one figure or two, or nothing?

At the open door, the wind on William's face had woken him fully and he decided to walk to the fields. He needed to take a close look at one of the Beths; she had a touch of mastitis. If the moon came out again, he'd see well enough. Anyway, he needed fresh air to clear his head, and try to decide what he should do about Nancy. He grabbed an old coat off the peg and gave a whistle for the dog, who crept closely at his heels as they moved out of the yard, delighted at the thought of a walk.

The wind funnelled up the valley from the south. On the Cornish bank above the river, two khaki-clad men manned the searchlights. It was an exposed position, up there at the top of Pentillie Lawns. They were not really lawns, but fields that grew the earliest grass on the western bank of the Tamar. They turned up the collars of their khaki overcoats and waited. On the wind came the noise of heavy bombing. The men were enfolded by the darkness. They felt lonely and frightened as they looked across at the valley devoid of electric light.

Meanwhile, on the Devon side of the river, the Americans stood beside their anti-aircraft guns, and they waited too.

If a German plane should be forced to climb away from the flak of the well-defended dockyards before it had dropped all its bombs, the pilot would be forced to pull out to the north. Following the route of the river and safely away from the gunfire around the port, the bombs would be unleashed before the aircraft headed back to Germany. This had happened enough times to leave pockmarked craters in the fields of the valley. A few times, the bombs had dropped into the river.

The army was wise to the enemy's tactics and the new anti-aircraft gun position had been strategically placed at Higher Birch. The searchlights at Pentillie Lawns would try to catch the plane in a beam of light so the guns on the Devon bank could take aim.

Out in the field, William viewed his cattle. At first glance, all looked peaceful. The bombardments in Plymouth had become so regular that now the cows simply chewed their cud and took no notice. However, the usual smell of seaweed and salt was mixed with the smell of burning – not the seasonal scent of bonfire but harsher altogether. Billowing red clouds were heaped up over Plymouth.

Then it came. The low, thundering noise of a damaged plane struggling to climb, desperate to escape the anti-aircraft flak coming at it from both sides of the river. William watched it slowly pull away from the mayhem and head straight towards him. He somehow sensed that it had one more bomb to drop before limping home. He thought, not of himself, but of his dear innocent cows and then of Nancy, probably by now back in the farmhouse. He swore and prayed and flung himself onto the ground. The plane screamed over his head. The cattle were up and milling around, distressed by the angry ear-splitting noise. Over it came and on, then a huge explosion, followed by a roar. It had dropped its bomb and William could hear the sound of the aircraft as it dragged its injured body onwards, desperate to limp home to Germany. The 'all-clear' sounded in the distance.

William stumbled to his feet and rushed forward. Rounding the bend in the green lane, he saw that the house was safe but the barn was ablaze. He ran to the stables, coughing and spluttering in the swirling smoke, and flung wide the doors. The horses plunged and strained against their halters. William reached into his pocket and with trembling hands he struggled to slash through their ropes and release them from their stalls. They pushed violently past him, nearly knocking him over, before galloping off and standing at a distance with heaving flanks and wild eyes. Now he rushed back and forth trying to pull clear the bags of grain, but the heat was intense.

By now a small crowd from the village had gathered and a few able-bodied neighbours formed two lines, one to pull clear sacks of grain, harnesses and anything else they could salvage, another to pass buckets of water to dampen down the ground and stop the fire spreading to any other building. They laboured for hours working as a team, silent and shocked. But the last section of straw went up and the heat drove them back. They had at least stopped any other building catching fire. Finally, the barn that had taken so long to build and so little time to be destroyed was burnt out and left smouldering.

"Lucky it didn't catch the ricks," Walter said, trying as always to look on the bright side.

"Come in and quench your thirst," William muttered, his shoulders drooping in despair as he led the helpers back to the house. The oil lamp was burning, but there was no sign of Nancy. He bounded upstairs, shouting as he went.

"Nancy, Nancy, where are you?" Panic started to take hold of him.

"Where the hell is she?"

Downstairs, his neighbours were looking embarrassed, their faces grimy from the firefighting. They muttered among themselves.

"Anyone seen her this evening?" William asked the assembled company. Walter was the first to speak.

"My missus saw that Yank walking past our cottage with her. They seemed to be on their way to the farm. It was about an hour before the bomb dropped."

William tried to work out what could have happened. Surely, even Nancy would not have brought the Yank to the house. Suddenly, he thought of the barn and rushed back outside. One end still stood at a crazy angle. Everything was glowing with heat and to try to get nearer would have been madness. Nothing could have lived inside the charred interior. William turned around.

"Thanks for your help. I'll have to wait till morning. If you see her, let me know."

But in his heart he knew, and they knew too. It was common knowledge; they had seen her in the pub sitting far too close to the American and they had seen them walking in the moonlight with arms linked. The little gathering trooped off towards the village.

Next morning at first light, William went out and stared at the mess that was left of his new barn. The end that had housed the corn and the straw was burnt to the ground, but the other end had one heavy beam still in place and some of the sidewall. It was from here that Walter appeared. Dear, faithful Walter.

He had been pretty sure what he would find and he had been right.

"Don't you go in there, boss. Keep away."

"Nancy? The Yank too?"

"'fraid so." Walter rested his gnarled old hand on William's shoulder and walked with him back into the farmhouse and pushed him gently into the armchair.

"The shame of it." William sat with his head in his hands.

6

All Nancy's belongings were gathered up by Edna, scooped into a trunk and stored out of the way. Her body, what was left of it, was cremated. The ashes in a marble urn were sent by William to a northern town with a letter briefly explaining the circumstances but omitting any mention of the American. Nancy had hardly mentioned her family and William sensed that there was no love lost between them. Elsie had told him that Nancy had been very unhappy at home and her parents both drank and were abusive. Now only the lingering smell of her perfume hung on in the farmhouse. After a while this too disappeared and William carried on as if nothing had happened, working as hard as ever, insulating himself from the world beyond the farm gate, becoming silent and withdrawn.

The war in Europe and the Far East dragged on.

Edna worried about William. She tried to engage him in the drama of what was happening, even asking her niece Florence to buy him a cat's whisker wireless from Exeter, where she was working. Among the squeaks and interference William made an effort to keep up with the news. The routine of his life became burdensome.

*

By 1944, Devon and Cornwall were full of American, New Zealand and Canadian troops. They had taken over airfields and camps. The villages reverberated with the sound of their strange voices, and the locals were surprised by their relaxed manners. At the coast, there was great activity. Sometimes, rigid raiding and landing crafts would come up the Tamar. The residents felt a mixture of fear and excitement when they saw these menacing machines manned by men in helmets or balaclavas, their faces blacked out. They came by night, often coinciding with military manoeuvres on the land. A feeling of anticipation hovered everywhere.

For William, lambing was coming to an end and out in the fields each dawn he was busy carefully walking round, his eyes skimming across the flock, aware of any lost lambs or ewes caught in brambles, and making sure that no sheep were lame. The exhaustion of nights spent in the lambing shed slowly lifted and on these early mornings he would hear the curlews calling on the estuary mud, see the lapwings tiptoeing through the fields, notice the many cobwebs spread across the grass and watch the last bats fluttering to their roosts. For a moment world events would recede.

One night William was out in Riversedge hiding in the hedge, hoping to put an end to a persistent fox that was taking the weakest lambs. Wrapped in his old green jacket, he kept the twelve-bore out of sight in case the moonlight glinted on the barrels. He climbed up into the hedge, squatted in the undergrowth on top and, motionless, he waited patiently.

He was stiff and uncomfortable. Half an hour passed with nothing but the odd rabbit hopping by, oblivious to his presence. Suddenly, William heard a twig crack. Careless fox, he thought. Gently, he slid the gun up to his shoulder and cocked it. He had heard the noise just behind him, so he aimed along the side of the hedge and waited for the animal to follow his usual path up and through the blackthorn. He knew there was a fox run there; he'd seen the tiny red hairs left on the thorns as every night this creature of habit had squeezed through. This one was making more noise than normal: must be a big one, or injured in some way. He braced himself and adjusted the stock closely into his shoulder. From the top of the hedge leapt a camouflaged figure, definitely not a fox. The sheep scattered, and William let out an oath. He uncocked the gun and jumped down. The soldier whirled round.

"Bloody hell, what the blazes are you doing here?"

"Well, it's my farm," William said defensively.

He was stiff from crouching in the hedge for so long and rubbed his hands together, moving from foot to foot.

"You cold, mate? Here, have a drop of this."

The soldier fumbled in the inner pocket of his battledress and produced a hip flask. William was not a drinking man and the strong liquor burned his throat, but he immediately felt warmed and studied his companion as closely as he could in the half-light. He was bundled up in so many clothes it was difficult to make out his features; a balaclava was rolled up around his ears and his cheeks were blackened by camouflage. He had lanky long legs and his wrists showed below his sleeves.

"You're an Australian?"

"No, no, definitely not, I'm a New Zealander, from North Island," he protested.

The flask moved back and forth between the two men as they stood close together in the gloom, hunched against the wind, exchanging a few details of their lives.

William learned his name was Frank Weld and he was on an exercise. Frank explained that his maternal grandfather had been in the Devonshires and because of this, he had been able to join the regiment. William also learned that at home on North Island Frank was a sheep farmer.

Frank glanced at his watch.

"I must go. If I'm still in the area at shearing time, I'll come and give you a hand."

He loped off across the field towards the river, unobtrusive in the half-light, but his long legs were easily recognisable. In the distance, William could hear a small but powerful engine – the pick-up boat, he thought.

7

Shearing time came early in the mild Tamar valley. Once again, William got out the wooden boards, sharpened the shears and prepared the holding pens. He had just driven the first bunch in with the help of old Tig when she started barking and he turned to see the lanky New Zealander striding into the yard.

"Good timing, Frank. I'm really pleased to see you."

"Let's have a go with those Devon hand-shears then, William. It'll be a treat for me. Too much hanging around these days. I need some action."

This was the first time William had seen Frank in daylight. He had such elongated legs, and the fact that his trousers were two inches too short exaggerated this. He was very slim and athletic with long arms to match the legs. The really startling feature was the intense blue of his eyes, like the periwinkles in the hedges. He would hold William's gaze intently and, more often than not, a big warm grin would engulf his features. He always seemed to be in a good humour.

The long hard day William had anticipated, all alone, catching each sheep, upending it, cutting away the old fleece, releasing each animal, laying down the shears, and finally rolling up the wool, did not turn out as expected. Usually Walter would have come in to roll the fleeces, but he had suffered one of his attacks of bronchitis. But thanks to Frank, things flowed fast and smoothly.

The first sheep was now swaddled in Frank's arms; within five minutes she was standing again, shorn and newly white, looking as amazed as William.

"You've done this before, haven't you? Thank God I didn't shoot you in that hedge." William felt his spirits rise.

So, all day long, the two men worked and chatted, each respecting the other's skills.

"Makes me feel less homesick, mate. It's so like North Island here."

"Well, you've cheered me up no end, Frank. On my own, this would have taken two days or more to do the lot."

"I shall be free the same day next week. Shall we tail the lambs then? They could do with dagging." Frank laughed as he eyed the filthy wool around the young lambs' backsides. Relief showed all over William's face.

"You know," Frank continued, "I have a connection with this parish. I was born in 1918 at the end of the war, but in 1917 my uncle from Wellington was killed right here in Bere Ferrers."

"Oh my, not that terrible train disaster? My father was there – he told me about it."

William remembered his father's last evening. The two of them sitting at the kitchen table, and how distressed the old man had been by what had happened.

"I often think of those poor young men. Such a waste," William murmured.

*

A few nights later when William was making one of his rare visits to the pub, he spied Frank and realised that he was not the only reason for the New Zealander's visits to the parish; nor was it to visit the memorial for the dead uncle. Frank was sitting in a dark corner seat with the prettiest girl in the village, Florence. William felt the slightest twinge of regret. He should have pursued that one. He greeted them both warmly and bought them drinks. The talk flowed easily. As he walked home in the moonlight he realised that Frank's timely appearance for shearing might have had something to do with Florence; she would have heard from her Aunt Edna that William was short-handed and mentioned it to Frank.

The next week, Frank was back. They got through the lambs at a fine pace. Edna had cooked a stew for tea and Florence brought it up. With William's cider to drink, they had a good meal; at last, the farm kitchen was full of laughter. William learned how Frank had signed up as soon as he could because the tie with Britain was very strong in his family and many of them had served in the Great War; only his uncle had not come back.

"What about having a go at those rabbits tonight, William?" William was delighted to repay Frank's kindness and they set off. Frank was armed with an old four-ten and William carried the twelve-bore.

As if they had known each other for years, they chatted comfortably until they drew near the warren on the high ground above the river. Since his friendship with Stan, William had not felt this easy with another person and he realised at that moment that his recurrent nightmares no longer bothered him. Frank fell into step beside him.

"Just like our place on North Island, makes me feel quite at home. Means a lot to me this, William. Thanks."

Over the next few weeks, they had one or two shooting expeditions, but cartridges were in short supply so every shot had to count. Edna was delighted and cooked rabbit pie, as did many others of William's acquaintance in the village. They were very pleased to have something to supplement their rations and it was a good way to repay kindness. For the first time since Stan was killed, William felt he had a friend.

Early one perfect May morning soon after this, the telephone rang.

"William, got a surprise for you. Could you be my best man at the registry office next Saturday? Very hectic here at the base at the moment. Don't want to let anything as good as Florence slip through my fingers."

"I'm most flattered to be asked. Of course." There was only a moment of remorse; it could have been different. But Frank would make Florence a good and kind husband and she'd see the other side of the world. William buried his regrets and prepared for the next weekend. The suit that had been his father's came out of the cupboard and was hung up in the yard to air to get rid of the smell of mothballs. Edna ironed his best white shirt with the greatest care and pressed his tie and handkerchief.

*

So it was on a Saturday morning in June that they gathered at the registry office in Tavistock, with the Stannary buildings towering around them and within sound of the River Tavy. A damp morning had given way to sunshine and the slate roofs glistened before the sun quickly dried them off. A few soldiers from the Devonshires came to support the bridegroom, and Florence looked as radiant as she had done that day in the hay fields many years before. She wore a cream silk drop-waisted dress that had been her mother's. She and Edna had been up late for many nights altering it. Florence had used her extra clothing tokens as a bribe to barter in exchange for yards of silk from an old parachute that the Tregonings had found in their fields and had no use for. Painstakingly, they had managed to lengthen the old dress, adding a frill around the hem and sleeves and putting pin-tucks here and there. Now it fitted perfectly. William had picked some cream roses from the garden of Hawcoombe and these Florence cradled as she and Frank stood in the doorway to have their photographs taken. William overheard her saying, "I am so happy, Frank."

He had winked at her.

"This is just the beginning, my very own Devonshire darling."

Watching them, William was happy for them both and kept any tinge of envy well hidden.

The two honeymooned at the Castle Inn, at Lydford. The next week, they were due to join William on the farm. But it was not to be.

A message came for Frank during their breakfast. There was an emergency. Frank was recalled to his barracks and rejoined his regiment later that day. Florence felt desperate; left alone, she packed up their belongings from the bedroom. All was so secret. It was war and she must understand and try to drive away her own selfish thoughts. She stood at the window, Frank's crumpled shirt in her hands. She buried her face in it and smelled his special smell. She watched a scowling cloud creep across the sun and shuddered with foreboding.

Frank was in the second wave of landings on Golden Beach. He drowned before he reached the shore.

8

Florence watched a ragged flock of lapwings flying an erratic route above the exposed mud, and then she heard, clear as a bell, the lilting sound of a curlew. She looked downstream to the Brunel Bridge and her thoughts travelled on, beyond the estuary to Plymouth Sound and out across the Channel.

With an ache in her chest, she pictured Frank jumping from the landing craft with his gun held high above his head, the huge pack weighing him down. He would have expected to feel firm sand under his feet. Before his eyes went below the waves, he'd have realised that he had been dropped too far out. His last look at the world would have been that beach, seen through a miasma of smoke. He would have seen the bodies piling up, the abandoned machinery, and he would have heard the roar of gunfire, deafening, hard, metallic and hateful. Then, under the waves, struggling, he would have dropped his gun and tried to wriggle out of the huge pack. Slowly, the crushing pain in his lungs would have made his frantic attempts to reach the surface more futile and he would have blacked out. He would have sunk, trapped by his heavy burden, onto the French sand.

Had he had a moment to think of her? Probably not. But every day for the rest of her life, Florence would think of him.

Her dear Frank with his long arms and legs, his blue eyes that would hold her gaze so seriously until suddenly, when she least expected it, they would turn into a wicked wink and a smile that would engulf her. That was happiness.

"Oh, Frank, how will I get through life without you?"

Florence wrote to Frank's people in New Zealand. The first letter was rather formal, but the reply she received was so full of warmth. His mother was thirsty for any knowledge of Frank's Devon life. So the two women started a regular correspondence. Florence learned of Frank's life as a small boy growing up on a sheep farm on North Island. His mother, in turn, heard of Frank's kindness, not only to Florence, but also to William.

9

A cold gust of wind from the south buffeted the farmhouse and with it came flurries of rain. Leaves swirled around in the semi-darkness. Reluctantly, William had left his seat beside the range. He had had a long day ploughing. Now he must see the heifer in the paddock. He wrapped an old sack around his shoulders for extra protection. It would have been a long walk out there without the tractor, which had been Frank's legacy. William had received a letter from a New Zealand lawyer to tell him of Frank's bequest. Before Frank had married, he had changed his will, and William had inherited enough money to buy the Ferguson tractor; Frank must have known the odds against his survival. William missed him.

William's reluctance to leave the warmth of the kitchen was replaced by anticipation of a new arrival. If Winnie had a bull calf, this could be the one to carry the herd forward. In the half-light, he picked out Winnie standing alone beside a thick blackthorn hedge, sheltering from the weather. The sound of his approach gave her no cause for concern; she knew his arrival generally meant hay and a scratch. He called gently to her as he approached and she obligingly swung her tail round towards him. Talking to her in a low voice, he went on scratching her and was relieved to see one white hoof had already appeared. He felt for the second. Nothing. Stripping off the sack and his old coat, William rolled up his shirtsleeve. He gently slipped his arm inside her and as she moved, restless now, he followed her. He felt about in the warm cavern and found the other foot. The leg was bent backwards. Expertly, he brought it forward. Now, two little hooves and a nose were all lined up for birth. He left her to settle again. For fifteen minutes he waited as the contractions grew stronger. She gave a great bellow. With the next contraction, he got hold of both slippery little feet and as she pushed, he pulled. Between them they did it. With a great torrent of liquid, the calf fell with a splash onto the ground. Steam rose in the cold air. William felt for the head and cleared mucus from the calf's nose and mouth. Finally, he reached down between its back legs. It was a bull calf.

The miracle of birth never left William. Winnie was making gentle, throaty noises to the calf, low and loving. It was a sound that William found very moving. Now he rose, retrieved his coat and sack and moved away to climb once more up into his tractor.

Although he had put great thought into the continuation of the herd, William had not given much consideration to what would happen after he died. Sitting there in the dark with the smell of the sea in the wind, he realised he must get on. He would be fifty soon and who would have him?

10

Florence was now working as a nanny for a doctor's family in Exeter. The one weekend a month that she had off, she spent with her Aunt Edna and Uncle Walter. Their kindness and simplicity calmed her. They asked no questions. When she came back in February, it was marmalade time and they would sit around the table, each with a pile of soft-boiled oranges in front of them. They would be bent to their work, chatting in low voices and slicing the rinds until their fingers were white and puckered. On the Rayburn, more pans of fruit were cooking. The smell was wonderful, sweetness combined with a sharp tang.

April brought lambing. Inevitably, a cardboard box would be set up on the rag rug in front of Edna's stove with a tiny orphan lamb in it, struggling for survival. This would be the frailest orphan from William's small flock. Edna and Florence would take turns feeding the lamb out of an old baby bottle.

In May, Florence would arrive to find their cottage filled with the pungent smell of elderflower. Dotted around every surface would be enamel bowls with flower heads floating on the surface of the sugary water. Each time Edna passed, she would stir the brew and send the flowers swirling around giving off more scent. By her next visit, all would be bottled and hidden in a cool shed out of the sunlight.

The soothing rhythm of the changing seasons helped Florence through her grieving for Frank. Each time she visited she would walk up the track to William's farm with marmalade, elderflower cordial, or to collect more milk powder for the lambs. On seeing her, William would feel a wave of happiness. They shared memories of Frank, and Florence would read the letters that she received from his mother in New Zealand. It was a relief for both of them to talk about him.

Very slowly and quietly, both came to look forward to the third weekend of every month. Sometimes, William would give Florence a lift down to the station. As the train drew out, he would start counting the days. He'd save the nicest jobs to do with her.

The weekend after the birth of Winnie's calf, William was hedging in Long Meadow. He loved the job and, as his father had too, he took great pride in having the tidiest stone hedges in the parish. The bigger boughs were piled up ready to be carried back to the yard and stored for fuel; the riggings were set to one side to be burned.

It was seventeen months since Frank's death. Slowly Florence was recovering. Her step quickened on this weekend as she walked across the field and saw William on the horizon, his arms full of branches.

The collie ran to greet her. Comfortable with Florence's presence now, old Tig no longer barked at her approach.

"Hello, William."

Florence wrapped her coat tightly around her and pulled her hat down around her ears.

"Good to see you, Florence. Cold? Just about to light the fire. That'll warm you up. There's three warmings with firewood. Cutting it down, carrying it in and sitting beside it. In fact, there are four, with the burning of the riggings."

Watching carefully, her back to the wind, Florence saw the big roughened farmer's hands as they gently gathered tiny bits of dried grass, then some larger ones, and finally twigs. He piled them up so the flames would move towards the heap. He struck a match and the brown grass caught.

"Now, maid. Not too much, but keep it fed. Small bits, a little at a time. I'll tell you when you can start putting on the bigger branches. When you do, lay them all the same way, with the bushy bits to the middle. Remember, the flame will move away from the wind, so keep fuel on that side."

With one match they had the start of a bonfire, and Florence soon felt her face glowing. Shedding coat and hat, she started to work hard to keep ahead of the flames. William was enjoying it too, and they worked on into the late afternoon until the sparks lit up the sky.

"Better than any Guy Fawkes' party. Best move your clothes back or they will be riddled with burn holes like a colander." Doing this, she spied a large rotted log and tried to lift it. William stooped to grab the other end and together they swung it into the centre of the flames, causing a great crackling and a myriad of sparks to dance upwards. Turning towards Florence, William noticed her flushed cheeks and saw her eyes on him. Moving close to her, he placed his hands on her shoulders and turned her towards him. Behind her, framing her head, the fire was aglow.

"We could have a grand time together, maid. Would you ever marry me? I know I can't replace Frank, but we could make a good life. Think about it."

Florence's voice was muffled as she buried her head in the tweed of his jacket. It smelled of woodsmoke.

"Yes, yes. I've already thought. Of course I will."

11

After completing the official part of the marriage in the Tavistock registry office, Florence and William had a blessing in the parish church of St Andrew's in Bere Ferrers. Finally they went back to the farmhouse, where Edna had prepared a great spread for the neighbours. For weeks she had been saving coupons and gathering vegetables and fruit from the farm kitchen garden. William had slaughtered a couple of lambs. The smell of roasting meat wafted through the farmhouse and there were murmurs of anticipation from the guests. The throng filled the kitchen and the parlour, and everyone enjoyed Edna's good baking and the roasted meat. Some remembered their last visit to the farm and the tragedy of Nancy and the American soldier in the barn. They were relieved that, at last, William's life was taking a turn for the better. Florence was a great favourite in the village. Finally they all left, a flurry of leaves swirling around them as they crossed the yard.

Within a short time, thankfully for William, life settled down. The days followed a pattern; only the seasons altered the tasks. They rose each morning after the news summary, and at nine thirty each evening, they would climb the stairs to their bed.

Florence came from farming stock. She understood the life that she had chosen; none of the excitement and adventures that might have happened with Frank would occur. But William was a good man, kind and dependable.

She was wise enough to move nothing and made only the slightest changes, and these very slowly. It was difficult to buy material or furniture, so she used her ingenuity. She painted some of the old, lumpy brown cupboards and chests of drawers in pastel colours, and decided she would make a patchwork quilt. She collected little scraps of cloth from discarded garments or leftovers from previous dressmaking projects. These she cut into squares and put into a large basket. During the evenings, she would sit at the kitchen table beside the Aga pinning and then tacking them together in great strips. William would sit at the other end of the big pine table with piles of paperwork around him, sometimes cursing the bureaucracy that was engulfing all farmers. Occasionally, he'd look up and, catching sight of one of the squares, would remember that surely it had been the material of Florence's haymaking bonnet? Then, he'd see a scrap from the bathroom curtains of years ago sitting nicely next to Old Tom's pyjama leg, cream with blue and red stripes. He would smile to himself.

The mornings had become quite chilly now and mist hung above the river. With the corn harvest over and the cattle still out in the fields, there was the slightest lull in the farming year. They started to feed hay to the animals, taking it out in a trailer. Bouncing along in the grey Fergie tractor with Florence perched on the wheel arch, sometimes they would talk and sometimes there would be just a quiet companionship.

"Stop, William. Look – don't drive over them." She jumped down and ran this way and that gathering mushrooms in her apron until it could hold no more. They nestled them into an old sack, and at lunchtime, Florence cooked them in butter; they were delicious.

The next morning, she was better prepared and took a flat basket and a knife. William laughed at her girlish enthusiasm. They set off early, Florence's eyes darting about.

"Don't pick the baby ones, and leave the old ones so the spores spread. Such a mystery. None for two years and now this!"

"I think you could spot a mushroom at fifty yards," laughed William.

"It's a miracle." For four mornings, they harvested the mushrooms. Then, one wet afternoon, William returned earlier than usual soaked to the skin by the deluge. The rain became heavier, followed by a rumble of thunder. Early darkness closed around them.

Sitting in the window seat, they watched the huge drops falling straight and heavy, bouncing up on the concrete of the yard. The valley lit up with sheet lightning, losing colour but not light.

"Ruin the mushrooms," said Florence sadly. She must tell him her secret, but felt shy.

"William, I've got something important to say." She paused, embarrassed, turning towards him. "I am going to have a baby."

He did not know what to do with his emotion. He felt tears in his eyes. Leaning forward, he took both her hands in his and sat like that for a while.

"This is a real blessing, my love. I am so happy."

Forty-three was a fair age for a first pregnancy but Florence was strong and fit. Luckily, she had very little sickness in the first few months. Later, she loved to put her hands on her stomach and feel the baby move. William tried hard not to show his pride, but every so often she'd catch him looking at her in a special way. Then he would come up behind her and cradle the baby in his big hands and feel the butterfly-like movements of the tiny creature. She began to long for the hour's rest that William insisted she take after lunch. She would lie on top of the bed looking out of the window, watching wheeling gulls and hearing the hum of the tractor in the distance. Outside was a huge pear tree, and as each day passed, more leaves drifted to the ground. William felt comfortable and great warmth for his dear wife. So their days gently unfolded and fitted into the rhythm of the farming calendar. The patchwork quilt grew in strips, expanding left and right. Florence now had to use most of the table and William had to move his paperwork tightly further up to his end. During lambing, she struggled, and in the evening William would glance at her and see her head drooping forward on the table and her hands at last at rest. He'd quietly creep behind her chair, gather her in his great arms and lift her to her feet.

"Time for bed, my girl," he would say and guide her up the stairs.

Florence was nearly at the end of the quilt-making. At the back of the ironing cupboard she found an old linen sheet, yellowed by age. She soaked it well, gave it many washes, rinsed it, and finally wrung it out through the mangle and pinned it on the line in the orchard. There it flapped among the apple trees. They were dropping with fruit this year, a glorious mixture of varieties, acid green Pig's Snout, red Worcesters and yellow Polly White Hair.

She stitched up the lining to the multicoloured patchwork and felt joy and pride as finally the quilt was complete.

"There, William, that will keep us snug this winter."

"You're a good girl, Florence. It's beautiful."

12

The pains were dull and distant at first but enough to wake her from her afternoon rest. Nothing, she thought. Florence drifted back to sleep. She woke to another contraction, sharper and more urgent. Only then did she begin to feel fear. She dragged her sluggish brain back to William's morning departure. Which field had he said he'd be in? She stood up and rather shakily headed towards the stairs. At the top, a pain made her catch her breath. She held tight to the banister and waited for it to pass. Downstairs again, she put the kettle on. It would be ages yet; she must be calm and patient. She heard the heavy resonant ticks of the grandfather clock. Now the sharp stabs were coming every seven minutes. They took her breath away. In between them, she kept moving carefully from room to room. Then she remembered that she had not put William's dirty work trousers to soak. In that moment it dominated her mind, and she went to the washroom to pull them from the pile. Lowering the two pairs below the surface of the soapy water, she gave them a swirl around. There. Now she was ready. But no William, and a good two hundred yards to Edna's cottage. As she walked through the parlour, quiet, dark and cool, a much greater contraction overwhelmed her and she slipped down to the floor, grabbing the smooth polished legs of the elm table as if her life depended upon them.

This is how William and Edna found her. As soon as she saw her large and dependable husband, Florence felt the responsibility for herself being passed to him. The panic left her. He spoke gently, and with Edna's help they got her back upstairs.

"Better move that quilt, hadn't we, my love," William said as he gently lowered her onto the iron bed. He left Florence with Edna, who had seen so many village babies into the world.

Back downstairs, William was glad to find Walter to divert him. They brewed some tea and the old man tried to distract him with tales of past agricultural adventures. William had heard them all before but appreciated Walter's presence and tried to concentrate. They were on their third pot of tea and were just draining their cups when Edna bustled in.

"What a hurry your son was in to get into this world." Her face was wreathed in smiles.

"Give me five minutes and then come up and meet him," she said.

"A son," whispered William.

13

Florence had always loved children. The sweet twins she had cared for had helped her through her mourning for Frank. But nothing prepared her for the swelling emotion she felt for her son. As she sat beside the Aga breastfeeding, he would suddenly look up at her with such adoration that she felt her heart contract with joy and pride.

Sometimes, William would arrive in the kitchen to find the smell of freshly baked loaves but no sign of his wife or his son. He'd creep upstairs to find Florence hanging over the cot watching the baby as he slept, the covers rising and falling. William and Florence would exchange a secret smile together and both would recognise this as happiness.

They christened the baby Tom following the family tradition of alternating the names William and Tom.

Tom grew into a strong little boy, crawling towards the door to greet William. Before long, his greatest treat became a ride on the tractor, tucked between the steering wheel and his father. Life for William had changed out of all recognition. It was only now that he realised how incomplete and lonely his world had been before. His life had purpose now: he could look forward.

*

Before many years Tom was joining in the farm work, helping bring in the cows, rolling the fleeces at shearing time and walking out to do the daily stock check. He learned to recognise a cow with mastitis or a sheep with fly strike. At lambing, his small hands would help with difficult deliveries.

Florence watched the two of them walking across the yard. Now Tom, at fourteen, was nearly as tall as his father. The hard physical work had matured him early; the two looked almost identical with the same stride and the same angle at the elbow; the legs too, were long, and they both looked loose-limbed. They dressed in the same leather belts, denim jeans and black rubber boots. At least she never had to sort the clothes into two piles – they were interchangeable.

In the evenings, while Florence cooked the supper, the two would pore over the *Farmer's Weekly*, discussing hydraulics and horsepower, their voices rising and falling. She felt at peace. The farm was prospering and a new four-wheel-drive Massey Ferguson had become a reality.

During harvest, William would get a local farm labourer, Bert Luxton, to help Walter with the tractor driving. He was obliging and would work whenever needed. As both William and Walter's health declined, Bert came more often. He would teach Young Tom how to build up the stone hedges, how to pick out the right shaped stones and how to cut the mixed growth on top with a billhook.

"Not right through, mind, leave enough for the sap to rise.

Lay it down, not too far, never below horizontal, and bend it over away from the sun so that when it shoots it will come up this way." He gestured. "And make a good barrier to keep the stock in. I hate this barbed wire, ever since my father told me stories about getting caught up in it in that dreadful war."

"Blimey! Did he really get caught in it? Tell me about it, Bert. I've just been learning about it."

"It was at Ypres in those bloody trenches. There was a push forward. The night before there'd been a huge bombardment to make sure the way ahead was as clear as possible. My dad's company went up over the top; right in front of them the wire hadn't been cut. Under heavy fire Dad tried to climb over the bloody thing. His foot slipped in the mud and he fell face down on top of it and was totally hooked up. He thought his end had come, poor sod. He decided to lie quite still, as though dead. The barbs were cutting into him, right through his battledress. Must have been like torture. His mates were dead or dying all around. After what seemed hours, his company was pulled back. Of course, he couldn't move. The worst thing was this dreadful sound. Thousands, yes, Tom, thousands of men, lying wounded, groaning and crying out in pain all bloody night. A sound he could never forget."

"My dad won't talk about it," muttered Tom. "Mother says I mustn't ask him. He had such a bad time."

Bert was sitting now, absorbed in his thoughts. Then he continued, "When it was dark, he started to disentangle himself. Imagine how difficult that was. He tore himself to shreds but somehow he did it. Bleeding and half naked, he struggled back to his unit. I remember seeing the scars – they were all over him."

"Did he fight in the last war?" Tom asked.

"No, he was in a reserve occupation, just like farming. Needed at home, see. Father was working in the dockyard. He did nights. Mother was home with three of us boys. When the siren went to tell us the Jerry bombs was on the way, she'd take us all down to this underground shelter. Don't know what it had been – some sort of tunnel. The smell was dreadful – fags, pee and smelly bodies. We hated it. We'd run wild, us boys. Mother would shout at us. We plagued everyone. They'd be trying to sleep and we'd be making a racket."

Bert pulled out his tin of tobacco and started to roll up a cigarette with his huge hands. The tiny, thin paper seemed so obedient and in no time became a perfect little cylinder. Flicking a lighter, he then drew on it with great relief.

"One night, the siren went off. Mother was pissed off with us. Couldn't face trying to keep us quiet down there in the shelter. So she pushed us all into the tiny cupboard under the stairs. It smelled of cleaning things and it was as dark as a cow's gut in there. I was sat on a huge tin of Mansion Polish. Brother Fred had a torch and we played snap until the all-clear sounded. At dawn, Father came off the night shift. He had spent most of it in the works shelter. He'd heard an explosion nearby. The area was in uproar: dust, fallen houses, rubble, ambulances, fire engines were everywhere. The tunnel we were meant to be in had taken a direct hit. No one got out alive. Father thought we'd all had it. He came home, and there we all were."

"Like the story of the goat and her kids," said Tom. Bert wasn't sure about this, but he nodded and drew in strongly on the last of his 'rolly', then ground it out in the soil and flicked it expertly into the hedge.

"Father looked at all those scars on his body and he saw the ruins of the streets where he had grown up, and he made a decision. That very day, he made us all pack up our possessions. Each boy wrapped up his bedding and clothes in a bundle made of old sheets. We took five chairs and a table and piled everything onto a handcart. We trundled it down to the station and caught the next train to Bere Ferrers."

Tom was all ears. "What happened then?"

"He must've known about this old boat pulled up on the beach, the *Merganser* – you know, the brown one down there. Well, we all went to live on it. Looking back, it was fun for us boys. We ran wild. But poor old Mother must have found it hard. It was so basic. At the end of the war, we just never went back to Plymouth. Mostly, we lived on salmon and rabbit."

He paused.

"Come on, boy, we must get on. What will your dad think, us sitting here, jawing."

Tom's respect for Bert grew daily and he encouraged him to tell more stories of his youth. He also learned a great deal – where the salmon lay, how to set a snare and how to work ferrets.

14

Each year as the autumn mists gathered in the valley, William's chronic cough would start. Florence would hear him fighting for breath. She would see fear in his eyes as he battled to get air into his gas-damaged lungs. Tom had long since taken over all the manual tasks. At the same time, the advent of so much mechanised farm machinery had lengthened William's usefulness and now he looked forward to the harvest and driving the new combine.

Perched up on the top of the huge machine, surrounded by levers, he would guide the header below him and watch it magically claw through the stalks of corn. Behind him, he could hear the grain piling up, and in his wake there was a long stream of straw. A miracle, all these tasks in one machine.

This year, 1967, William, seventy now, had needed a gentle push from behind from his son to help him clamber up the steep metal ladder to the open cockpit. He had sunk onto the driving seat and sat for a moment to regain his breath. The struggle was evident to Tom and Florence standing below with upturned faces.

"Careful on the steep, mind," called Florence. "I'll bring your pasty out at one."

The dew had now dried off and the field was perfect for harvesting. Tom was already on the tractor, towing the grain trailer and moving towards the top field.

The combine started up and William looked down at Florence. Not just a glance, but right into her eyes. He smiled and winked at her.

"See you later, love." He had looked so happy.

Florence, back in the dim light of the kitchen, covered the carcass from last night's meal with water, adding vegetables, then put the big stockpot on the hob to simmer. She worked through her tasks, pegging out the washing and feeding the fowls. She collected the freshly baked pasties from the larder, wrapping them carefully in greaseproof paper and placing them in her basket. She then brewed tea in the harvest kettle and with that in one hand and the basket in the other, she set off for the cornfield.

Lifting her feet high over the stubble, she half closed her eyes against the brightness of the sun. Beyond her, the river ran due north and a boat trimmed its red sails, tacking lazily upstream. The temperature was perfect. Thistledown floated past on the gentlest breeze. Tom had just driven past her, back towards the barns, with a fully laden grain trailer. He had pointed at the huge load and grinned at her. Prices were high and the yield was good.

She listened to the low rumble of the combine to judge where best to intercept William's passage around the field. Now the internal and deep-throated sound of the engine seemed to have been replaced by a rattily loose sound, open and agitated. The realisation that the combine had not yet appeared even though the engine noise had changed filtered into Florence's consciousness. Her step quickened. Coming to the brow of the hill, she saw the great green machine slumped on one side. The motor coughed and died. There was no sign of William. Her legs felt numb and jerky as she forced herself to run down the hill.

She saw his arm first, protruding from underneath. Bending to feel for his pulse, she realised that the whole weight of the axle was on top of William's chest, obscuring his face. He was trapped. There was no heartbeat.

Florence sat next to the still body. She knew there was nothing to be done.

She held William's big hand between both of hers and studied it, concentrating on this dear bit of him, trying to stop the warmth draining away.

It was quiet now, and high above her, a lark sang. She remembered how tenderly he had gathered the dried grass for that bonfire when he had proposed. She knew that it was the mixture of strength and gentleness that had captured her heart. She ran her fingers over the cracked, work-toughened skin of his palm. So many scars meeting and crossing, making a patchwork of struggle. The dam wall quivered; she could hold it back no longer. The first tear fell into the hollow of his hand.

There must have been a breakdown. William must have crawled under the machine to check the problem. The combine must have dropped down, pinning him to the earth and squeezing the breath out of his lungs. In these fields, there were many subterranean badger runs where the ground was likely to subside, invisible from high up on the combine.

Florence's grief was different this time. Not the turmoil of emotions that had accompanied the whirlwind marriage and sudden death of Frank. Florence's pain was so deep; it was the 'everydayness' of William that she had grown to love. That dear dependable presence was gone.

Young Tom found his mother sitting in the stubble field, holding the now cold hand of his father. Silent tears streamed down her face. She seemed to be in a place he could not reach.

"Mother, is he dead?" She had nodded her head and he had dropped down beside her, holding her hand, his other arm around her shoulders. They were sitting in the shade of the combine, the river below them. The serenity of an August afternoon fell around them. These were precious moments while both tried to come to terms with the tragedy. A slight breeze whipped up the empty cornhusks and, high above them, the skylark still sang, lonely and poignant. A butterfly settled on Florence's shoulder.

15

Tom moved first, breaking the spell and setting in action all the practical jobs that had to be done. He coped well for his fifteen years.

Edna, now an old lady, came to be with Florence and moved gently around the farmhouse, doing quiet useful things.

Bert came too when he was needed.

Somehow, they got through from one day to the next. The young collie, sitting beside the empty chair near the Aga, whined and looked around for her master.

"You sit there, Tom. I can't bear to see it empty." Mother and son had each other and much to keep them busy. Once again, the combine stood upright, and Tom had to climb up into the driving seat to finish the field.

Florence managed well at first, organising the funeral with Edna's help. She continued to handle all the paperwork for the farm. She placed an announcement in the obituaries column of the *Tavistock Times*. When she read about William's death in print, her loss suddenly felt real and final.

At the funeral, St Andrew's Church was packed with farmers from all over Devon and Cornwall; William had been well valued as a breeder of South Devon cattle and those farmers were there to pay their respects. The rest of the congregation consisted of neighbours, looking awkward in their best dark suits; many had known William all their lives. He had been a highly respected member of his community, reading in church, standing erect in his uniform for the Service of Remembrance around the war memorial, lending straw bales for village entertainments and helping his neighbours whenever his farm work allowed.

Florence loved the feeling of her son standing warmly next to her. She leaned just slightly towards him. A tremor seemed to pass through his body and she looked up at him and saw that he was struggling to hold back tears. 'Abide With Me', played at so many farmers' funerals, was too much for the young man to bear and she heard a strangled sob as he battled not to break down. Her Tom, so young to manage without his father; she too felt the tears running down her own face and felt in her pocket for her handkerchief and was glad to see Tom had found his. Together they fought their inner battles and managed to be under control by the time they finally followed the coffin and led the congregation out to the family gravestone overlooking the River Tavy. William was buried beside Old Tom and Agnes. The names on the stone, Tom, William, Tom were repeated in the same order back through the generations – all from Hawcoombe Farm in the parish of Bere Ferrers. A space had been left on the tombstone to add William's name. Just to one side was another stone, covered in moss. Frank Weld and then the dates. Florence felt a second wave of grief.

*

Over time Florence became stiff and brittle, retreating into her shell. Although neighbours and friends tried to comfort her she did not welcome their solicitude. She just wanted to be left alone and to wallow in her memories. She would wake each morning and stretch out her foot to find William's. A profound loneliness would overwhelm her, and she would muffle her sobs in case Tom should hear.

She felt that hard work was the answer, and she battled on, doing more on the farm, getting thinner, her face lined and drawn. This displaced, but did not dispel, her crushing sense of loss. Tom was kind enough but somehow it was as though each of them feared to know how much the other was suffering.

Autumn winds started to blow around the farmhouse and cold sleet lashed the peninsula.

"Do you think the cattle should come in, Mother?"

How should she know? William had made all the farming decisions. She must not show her uncertainty. Tom needed her support. She must be calm.

"Let's see what next week brings. The forecast sounds better. Dad tried to keep them out until the third week in October."

Tom seemed to grow daily, so much in the mould of his father except for his slim ankles and the shape of his hands, which were artistic, with beautiful nails, the quicks naturally showing perfect half-moons. Between the two of them, they managed to keep the farm going. Tom was glad of the new tractor; it speeded things up. They did not make money but neither did they lose it. The neighbours were kind and helpful, steering Tom in the right direction. A quiet voice behind him in the livestock market would urge him to bid up to so much, then whisper, "Leave it now."

Florence appeared to those around her to accept William's death stoically. In reality her grief grew inward, chilling the marrow of her bones. She felt so tired and always cold. She missed William in every moment of her day. She withdrew from life. She could face nobody. She began to spend many hours in her vegetable garden. Here, with her hands in the soil, she felt close to him. Greatly affected by the seasons, she, like the plants, seemed to shrivel and wither as the cold winds swept in and the rain beat against the farmhouse. She lost weight despite still eating well. Life became wearisome. Where before there had been excitement in the varying tasks, now there was a monotone greyness and she felt exhausted.

16

Mother and son had a struggle to get through that first winter without William and the next was hardly better, but Tom gained confidence and despite his youth seemed almost by osmosis to have learned from his father.

The cattle were Tom's greatest love. He spent hours in the sheds or fields closely scrutinising them and deciding on the best specimens; he enjoyed being in charge of the breeding programme. He bought the *Farmer's Weekly* and studied it each evening.

Florence was standing at the kitchen sink. It was now two years since William had died. She was daydreaming and watching the dawn creeping over the old farm buildings. She had already let the chickens out and the dog had found the first patch of early sun and was stretched out peacefully. If there could have been a moment that her grieving stopped, or at least found a comfortable place to rest, then this was it. She could see Tom now rolling a churn across the yard, his head of dark brown curls, his strong broad shoulders as he moved between sun and shadow, and in that moment she thought how lucky she was to have this son, this young man who was half her and half her darling husband. The beams of bright spring sunshine stole slowly around the yard and now as they reached the kitchen window she felt their warmth and half closed her eyes, allowing her body to relax. The bitter sadness seemed to ebb away.

Florence came to realise that both she and Tom had cut themselves off, like animals licking their wounds. It was time they reconnected with the world, or at least the village.

"It's about time you got out and about instead of poring over the farming press every night, Tom. What about visiting the pub? You might hear what is going on with Warren Farm too."

Next door to Hawcoombe was this tenanted farm that had remained empty since the incumbent farmer, Old George, who was a fair age, had had a heart attack. He had been a bit of a hermit and their only contact with him had been a hand held up in greeting if they passed one another. He had no relations who wanted to carry on the tenancy. The landlord had decided to sell and before Michaelmas there was to be an auction. The land was steep and much of it wooded, but it would be a natural expansion of Hawcoombe.

Florence was a little worried that Tom's life had become so solitary. He'd left school as soon as William died and had no interest in anything beyond agriculture. He had few friends, and certainly no female ones. All those years ago Florence had given William a wireless, and he had listened each night to the six o'clock news and then the news at ten before damping down the Aga and heading for bed. Tom, on the other hand, had closed his young mind to everything except the farming life. Now, at nineteen, it was high time he got out and about. Florence thought he might feel guilty leaving her alone if he headed off to the pub but she encouraged him: "It'll give me a chance to read my book. Off you go."

Tom shifted in his seat and turned to look at Florence. It was the first time she had shown any interest in anything beyond the farm.

In the Old Plough Inn the farmers' sons would gather. Endlessly, they would talk of new agricultural machinery as they rocked back and forward on the balls of their feet, their none-too-clean hands clasping beer glasses. Each night, they would form the same crescent around the bar, standing always in an identical formation. As they grew older, the chat would turn to 'females' as though they were talking about their stock. Florence would have winced if she had heard such talk. Only half joking, there would be a reference to how many acres the girls' fathers owned. This was primitive stuff, but Tom laughed and joined in.

At breakfast after one of these evenings, Tom and Florence were sitting in the farm kitchen. "One egg or two, Tom?"

But Tom was miles away thinking of what he had heard at the bar the night before.

"The agents are talking about a crazy price for Warren. It's that house that is pushing the value up – it's got a wonderful view. It'll be way beyond anything we could afford, Mother. Probably be turned into a gentleman's residence and the land will be left to go to pot. But I'll find out more tonight."

Next morning mother and son sat in the farmhouse kitchen. Tom was eager to talk.

"Mum, there's someone after Warren Farm already. Bill's sister works in the agent's office. An old chap, he really only wants the farmhouse – maybe we could do a deal."

Florence pushed a thick slice of toast across to Tom.

"I don't know, Tom. Do we really want that bit of land? It is so steep and there is talk that it has had red water for years – we don't need that in our cattle. We are managing as we are."

"To survive we have to get bigger, Mother. That is the way it is going."

It took all Florence's courage to ring the agent and suggest that they might buy the land at Warren Farm, and that a better price could be achieved if the house were sold as a separate transaction. The agent jumped at this. Then he said, "But of course, you must know who is buying the cottage. He says he is your brother-in-law. Albert Northwood."

The agent was new to the job and did not know the area or any of the local gossip. He had no idea how shocking this bit of news was to Florence. She stumbled through to the end of the conversation, replaced the receiver and turned to Tom, white-faced.

"Albert, your uncle, is alive. He's the man buying Warren."

Tom hadn't heard much about Albert; his father had been rather reticent about his brother and anyway he had died at the Battle of the Somme.

"He died in the Great War, didn't he?"

"No, Tom, he was missing, presumed dead. After seven years, if nothing is heard, you become legally deceased. He must be seventy-four now. He was two years older than your father."

The harsh rasp of the telephone interrupted them. It was the agent again.

"Just been in touch with Albert Northwood. He is keen on your idea of splitting the property and a reduction in the house price, so now we just have to agree the value of the land. Perhaps we need to meet at the property tomorrow."

Next day Florence and Tom walked up the muddy track towards Warren. There had been heavy rain and the overgrown laurel was so bowed down it gave only just enough space for them to walk in single file and rain dripped on them as they pushed through. Tall poplars and ash had risen high above the little farmhouse, blocking out the light, and fallen apple trees were covering the lawn.

"Must have been lovely in its day," Florence said as she bent to pick a sweet chestnut from the ground.

Tom sounded enthusiastic.

"I suppose with a bit of hedge-trimming and some paring back the place could be tidied up. But that is not our worry. Let's look at the land and the hedges."

They turned off into the first little orchard and walked on together from one field to the next.

"Old George seems to have just let it all go, but I reckon it would not take much to get it back into good shape. Maybe just put sheep in to tidy it up and then have a go at the hedges next autumn. What do you think, Mother?"

Florence felt a little wave of happiness. It was going to be a project. Something new. She loved the little orchard. The old trees could do with a good prune but the orchard faced south and felt neither too dry nor too wet.

"Let's do it, Tom. The agent will be here in a minute. We'd better decide our top price before he comes."

Tom pulled out an old envelope from his pocket and a stub of pencil. He scribbled some figures down and showed Florence the total.

"That is our absolute limit. Will you do the talking, Mother? If he tries to push you up I'll just say, 'sorry, too much,' and start walking away."

"All right, Tom. Look, here he is."

The agent did not want the trouble of holding an auction or all the complications of parking cars, dragging out machinery and providing a mobile office. It took very little time for them to come to a mutually agreeable price, quite a few thousand less than the pencilled scribble on the old envelope.

"I'll now contact Mr Northwood and come back to you when I know that part of the deal has been finalised," the agent said. "He'll be pleased to get everything concluded and move in." Before he turned to leave, Florence asked if he could tell her the date that Albert would be arriving.

"I'll give you a ring and let you know." The agent revved the engine and the wheels spun in the wet grass. He gave a wave and drove off, splattering his vehicle with mud.

17

The night before Albert's arrival, Florence was unable to sleep. She felt unsettled and tossed and turned. The full moon lit the room and outside she could hear the eerie bark of a vixen calling to her mate. She went to the window and pulled back the curtain just in time to see a shooting star and, seconds later, another. She felt deeply uneasy about Albert and his reappearance, and his motive for buying Warren. The following morning she woke feeling rather low and crumpled by lack of sleep.

At the station, Florence stood partially concealed behind a pillar. Nervously she ran her tongue over her dry lips and watched the train as it came to a hissing halt. The doors swung open with a clunk. Out jumped a young man struggling with a bicycle, then a smartly dressed woman carrying a briefcase. Finally, a huge suitcase was pushed through the doorway and lowered gently onto the platform. She still held back, watching. An elderly, portly man clambered down, nervously stepping over the gap. The guard slammed the doors.

"Stand back, sir, we're off."

Albert stood on the empty platform, the fluff of seeding herb willow blowing around him. Florence stepped forward, trying to hide her horror at seeing her brother-in-law now turned into an old man. He was stooped over his luggage, attempting to clasp the flattened handle of his case. Once he had it firmly in his grip he straightened, but something in that stretch made Florence realise his back was hurting. She approached tentatively. Albert had become stout and his florid face was covered in broken veins. His nose was bulbous and a few stray grey hairs grew from his nostrils. His ears too were tufted like a squirrel's. He seemed much shorter than she remembered him.

Having good manners, Florence now had to hide any revulsion she was feeling. She forced a smile and held out her hand. "Albert, how lovely to see you."

So trite and so untrue. She wondered how she appeared to him. Did he see the grey wings in her hair? Did he notice that her body looked shrunken in too big a suit of skin? Did he see the lines of hardship and worry? She held out her hand, work-worn and reddened. But he lurched towards her. Florence smelled a whiff of alcohol and bad breath; she had already noticed his yellow teeth, unhappily arranged.

"Florence, my beauty, the same as ever. What a treat to see you again."

He ignored her outstretched hand and folded her against his mackintoshed paunch, planting a kiss on her resistant cheek.

She picked up his holdall and Albert carried his suitcase. They walked towards her Morris Minor. Florence realised by his wheezing breath that he was struggling with the case, so she dropped her hand to help. He immediately looped a finger over hers. She quickly managed to extricate herself and between them they lifted the case into the boot.

"Kind of you to collect me – thank you, my dear."

She was not 'his dear'.

"I've laid the tea and Tom should be back from market by now. I hope you are hungry. I've got a brisket in the oven."

"I have not had one of those since my days on the farm. South Devon beef, I imagine?"

"Oh yes, we kill the odd bullock for ourselves. Tom loves brisket."

He laughed rather derisively. "Tomorrow I will take you out for a slap-up meal. Anywhere decent around here?"

Florence had not been out for a meal for years. She thought hard.

"The Bedford Hotel in Tavistock is nice and near."

Even in this short exchange, she felt defensive about her beef and for the area. Keeping quiet, she negotiated the potholes skilfully, swinging into the yard and coming to a halt suddenly, pulling on the brake with force. No Land Rover, so Tom was not back yet. The geese gave their usual greeting.

Albert leaned back, making the car seat creak under his weight.

"Still got those bloody birds. They used to chase me across the yard. I hope you have got this lot under control."

Climbing out, he kicked in the direction of the gander, who was waddling towards him, neck stretched out and hissing.

"They won't hurt you, Albert. Just ignore them. I've shut the dogs in but you'll have to meet them in a moment."

It was not going smoothly. Albert was so unlike her William. She should have remembered this from her childhood.

For a moment she pictured her husband appearing from the stable, calling out a greeting to her.

Everything Albert said seemed to have a tinge of criticism about it, or was she being overly sensitive?

To Florence's eye her kitchen looked so inviting; late-flowering roses from the garden on the trestle table, which was laid for tea, the well-polished dresser full of Northwood china passed on from generation to generation, and old rugs on the floor partially covering the shining slates. But Albert just grunted, "So dark in here, you must need the electric lights on all day long."

Florence ignored this and showed him upstairs to his old room that she had aired and carefully prepared for him. Pushing open the door, she twitched the crease out of the yellow candlewick bedspread. Standing back, she expected some exclamation of surprise as he saw the newly painted walls and the thick rug spread over the old oak boards. But Albert just sank down on the bed, ruffling the covers.

"Have you put another bathroom in or do I still have to walk along the passage?"

"It is as it was but it isn't very far and there is lots of hot water. Tea will be ready in fifteen minutes." Florence ran down the stairs back to the kitchen and let out a deep breath. She felt desperate and hoped Tom would not be too long.

The brisket came out of the oven surrounded by root vegetables from the kitchen garden; it smelled pungent with goodness.

Albert appeared just as Tom entered.

"Tom, this is your Uncle Albert."

"Hi, nephew. You look just like your old dad, very agricultural."

From the way he said this Florence was sure it was a criticism not a compliment.

Tom did try to make conversation, but every topic he brought up Albert capped with tales of bigger and better, and of how easy life was in the States. They were on to the raspberries and cream when Tom asked, "Well, Uncle, if America is so fine, what interests you about Warren Farm? It has not been any more modernised than Hawcoombe has."

Albert rose from his chair. "I was born here, you know. Enough of that, I'm worn out. I'm going up to bed."

Next day Tom took Albert off in the Land Rover to look around the stock. The old man returned, once more exhausted, and said he needed a rest to recover from his jetlag. Before he disappeared up the stairs he asked to use the telephone and booked a table for two for eight o'clock that night at The Bedford. Florence's first thought, however, was would she be able to stay awake until the end of the meal; nine thirty was her bedtime.

When Tom came home his mother told him about her dinner with Albert.

"Find out what he is up to. I don't trust him."

Florence pulled out the old dress she usually wore under her big coat for funerals. It seemed rather tired, but she pinned a brooch on, and strung her mother's pearls around her neck. That would have to do.

Albert was waiting for her.

"It's not just a decent meal you need. You need to be taken shopping and bought some new clothes."

Florence ignored this and busied herself clattering the dogs' bowls and tipping out their biscuits. But she was amazed how rude he was.

Sitting in the formal dining room of The Bedford Hotel, Florence tried to relax among all the starched linen, the scrape of chairs and the murmur of voices. She felt slightly sick after three courses, all containing a great deal of cream. They had made small talk and now he excused himself and stumbled off towards the gents, knocking a chair over on his way. She felt trapped in such unfamiliar surroundings and her eyelids were getting heavy. She was not up to the conversation that she could see looming. Albert returned. He'd combed his thinning hair across his scalp and after the red wine he had drunk, his face looked red and blotchy. Florence cupped her only glass of wine between her hands. He leaned forward in his chair, took her glass and held her fingers in a firm grip. She noticed the hairs on his pudgy fingers.

"Now, Florence, this is my plan. You are still relatively young, well, many years younger than me. I could make the rest of your life really comfortable. I expect you and Tom have realised that I will be claiming my half of the farm. It is my inheritance."

Shocked, Florence tried to wrestle her hands out of his grasp.

"Just wait a minute. We could make this less painful if you will just listen to my plan. First, you know I have always fancied you. I still do."

With a visible shudder Florence remembered him as the surly boy on the school train who always tried to sit too close to her.

"In some cultures," he leaned back, sounding pompous, "a widow marries her brother-in-law as a matter of course. My suggestion is this. We marry. We go to live at Warren Farm, which I will make so smart and easy to run for you. We could have holidays together. You've hardly seen the world. I'll buy you new clothes, anything you want. We leave Tom at Hawcoombe and hope he soon finds himself a wife. He goes on farming both holdings."

Florence felt frozen with horror, only managing a negative grunt and a shake of her head.

"The alternative is not so funny, Florence. I take my half, which will force a sale, and you and Tom will be out of Hawcoombe by the end of the year." He snapped his chair forward and reached out to stroke her face. Florence recoiled and avoided the caress.

"That's the deal."

Florence sat quietly, hands now folded in her lap well out of Albert's way. She had moved her chair slightly back so he could not touch her. She looked serene but this gave no indication of what was going on beneath the surface. Her mind was racing but all she said was, "We'll see about that, Albert."

This was not the reaction Albert had expected. He felt nonplussed and impotent in the face of such calm. It was like the air leaking out of a balloon. There was an awkward silence. With the meal ended and the bill paid, they collected their belongings. Albert began to realise that this timid little woman whom he thought so subservient was not as she seemed.

*

On the drive home Florence had to endure the weight of his hand on her knee. She felt the sweat from his palm seeping through the thin material of her dress. Without being rude, she tried to think of some way to get him to remove his hand. She needed to divert him.

"There is a map in the side pocket. Have a look – you will be able to see that the expected extension of the railway never actually happened."

She continued talking about the train service and its threatened closure and how this might be the final death knell for the horticultural industry of the peninsula.

It seemed a long journey home. Once back, Florence busied herself with shutting the dogs away and turning off electric lights. Then, quickly, she was on the threshold of the stairs and bidding Albert a hasty goodnight and thanking him for dinner. Once in her bedroom she closed the door and quietly pushed the bolt across.

She then lay on top of the old quilt, thinking quietly. Tomorrow she would ask Albert about his life from that day on the Somme until today. Once she had heard his story she would work out what to do next; some detail of his life might work in her favour.

She heard the creak of the floorboards as Albert fumbled his way down the passage; he tripped on the rag rug, cursed, but then, finally, all was quiet and dark.

Albert rose late the next morning and sat in the kitchen eating his bacon and eggs. He tore off a piece of toast and chased every trace of yellow yolk around the plate meticulously.

"That has cleaned it all up," said Florence as she cleared the table.

"Well, once you have been nearly starved you never leave a crumb."

This was the opening Florence needed.

"Could you tell me about it, Albert, I mean…after the battle. After the Somme."

Albert took a long swig of tea.

"I could try." He rattled the cup back in the saucer. His bombastic self-confidence drained away. Slumped in his chair, he began.

"It was the hopelessness that overwhelmed me. Always cold, always wet. Those behind me jostled me up the ladder. Dragging ourselves uphill towards the German trenches through slippery mud, the noise, you could never imagine the noise. It was like hell. I just could not bear it any more. My body would not respond and then my brain would not either. Instead of going straight ahead, I began to head off at an angle. It was not a thought-out action. I was revolted by the whole thing. I stumbled on not firing, not thinking, always veering left. I didn't care any more. I seemed to have shut down. It was as if the noise were coming from somewhere else, the shouts, and the smell of cordite. I kept tracking left, nothing touched me. I felt unearthly…But you don't want to hear all this."

"Go on, Albert."

"I just kept going, kept west. Towards the sunset. Nobody challenged me. It was as though I had become invisible. Night fell, dawn came. I stumbled on and on. The mud slowly thickened and then I could see grass beneath my feet. The landscape changed from battlefield to farmland and a rough road took me into a small valley. I saw a cow grazing and beyond it a tumbledown cottage. I walked up the path, still off my head. Starving of course. The door was hanging on the top hinge, but I knocked. Very slowly, the door opened and a terrified woman peered out, her eyes wild. I broke down, wept. She took my arm and led me inside, bolting the door behind me. That's where I stayed for the rest of the war...We shared terror. Her husband had been reported missing, presumed dead, a few months earlier. We shared hunger. I helped by milking the cow – that much I remembered from Hawcoombe. We took some comfort from each other's bodies. Her name was Monique. By the time the war ended she was pregnant. I had learned French of a sort from her, rough and heavily accented but enough to get by. I took on her husband's identity. All his papers were in his chest of drawers upstairs. It seemed the easiest thing to do. I got a job in a local factory. Mostly I was mute. Nobody asked any questions. The war had thrown up plenty of odd behaviour. Once the baby was born, she sat with him on her knee and sobbed. On and on she cried. When she stopped, the baby would start. There was nothing I could do. Now I understand that she had post-natal depression but at the time..."

Albert stopped and looked up at Florence.

"I ran away again."

She topped up his teacup.

"The factory where I worked had promoted me. They were starting up in the States. They asked me to go with them. It seemed like a lifeline. I put some money on the sideboard in the cottage and left. Never even said goodbye to Monique and the baby. Couldn't face it."

He paused, looking stricken.

"But things got better then. Chicago was bustling with life and I made a success of the job and before long was assistant manager. We were making steel girders. Not exciting but it sure was profitable. I bought a house and sort of settled. I was earning good money and saved every penny I could. While the war continued in the East we were busier than ever making armaments. But I was doing a bit of bootlegging on the side and that brought in serious money. That is why I can afford to buy real estate here and live well."

As he spoke the last sentence Albert seemed to regain his confidence and sat up straighter in his chair.

"Oh, Albert. What a time you have had."

Florence sat silently. Could she believe a word he said? She had been ready to hate him. She was unprepared for the wave of sympathy that she now felt. She could imagine how it had been. She could understand why he had fled, not once but twice. Now he stretched his hand across the table to her and she gave it a squeeze of understanding. Getting to her feet, she gathered up the washing basket, intending to hang the contents on the line. But Albert said, "Wait a minute, don't rush off. Have you thought about the deal I was prepared to make? It was not offered lightly. I have booked a taxi to visit my lawyer in Plymouth tomorrow. Before then I need to know what you want to do. You know my plane is booked for Tuesday and I will be dealing with the purchase from Chicago."

Florence wished she had not given his hand a squeeze, wished she had kept her distance. Now she turned, the full basket of wet clothes heavy in her arms.

"It is a huge decision to make. I need time to think about it."

Albert struggled to his feet and raised his voice. "I'm too old to wait around. I need to know."

He moved off towards the stairs. Florence went out, the bright autumn sunshine dazzling her after the dark of the kitchen.

"How long is Albert staying, Mother?"

Although Tom was out in the fields hedge-trimming, ploughing and doing all the autumn jobs, he felt uncomfortable having his uncle in the house. He hated coming into the kitchen and finding Albert sitting in what had been his father's chair and he did not like the way he shoved the dogs away with a sly kick.

For some reason that Florence did not quite understand she had not told Tom about the deal. She felt embarrassed. This was a problem she was going to have to solve on her own. She made light of her reply.

"It won't be long: it is the least we can do, Tom. I know he has a return ticket for Tuesday and it is a long and tiring flight. Here, don't forget your flask for crib."

Returning to the kitchen, she found Albert sitting at the table.

"You made your mind up yet?" he barked.

"Oh, Albert, just leave it will you. Do what you have to do."

She sounded tired, but somehow her demeanour had changed. She bustled out of the kitchen into the hall and went to hang up her coat.

When she returned she said, "I don't think you will get anywhere with your lawyer. You have lost your identity. Who will believe you? Go and find out and get it out of your system, but I'm not marrying you or anyone else. You would be best to go back to America, where you keep telling us everything is so fine."

With that Florence went off upstairs to get on with her housework.

Albert's departure was as awkward as they had expected. Once he knew that his bullying was not going to get him anywhere he became morose and it was with great relief that Florence put him on the train on the following wet morning, the platform gleaming in the downpour. He did not try to kiss her. That was a relief. They parted with tense civility. The train door clunked shut with finality and Florence waved as the train wound around the corner. He had not remained at the doorway but had quickly withdrawn to his seat.

18

The sale of Warren Farmhouse now fell through but the idea of splitting the land and selling the house separately appealed to the agent. Eventually, another buyer turned up and Tom and Florence were delighted to finish the transaction and expand their acres. Florence never told Tom how Albert had tried to blackmail her. For the next two years, at Christmas, a card from Albert would arrive at Hawcoombe Farm. It had a Chicago postmark but no address for them to send a card back. After those two years no word was heard of him. Slowly Florence's worries faded as they heard nothing from Albert's lawyers. Maybe he had died. Sometimes she felt sorry for him but she tried to push these feelings away.

The new land gave both Florence and Tom a fresh interest and they talked during each meal of how best to amalgamate the two holdings.

"I could increase the herd, Mother. Bring more stock to finished weight. That would give a bigger income."

The cattle were Tom's greatest love. They were responding slowly to Tom's breeding plan.

The farm seemed to be doing well but to increase the stock

and improve the machinery they needed to raise substantial capital from the bank. For the moment Tom put this off, hoping he could manage without borrowing any money.

Florence loved the new acres: unlike Hawcoombe, the fields at Warren were within their original boundaries. She helped Tom and Bert build up the stone hedges and cut the growth on the top. They left the best boughs. These they bent over horizontally, always towards the south so that when they sprouted a thick stock-proof barrier would form, making this an excellent boundary for the cattle without using any wire. The rest were piled up for burning. Florence's job was to haul the branches to one side ready for the fire and then to tend it. She remembered William's proposal beside the bonfire, the smell of it and the myriad flecks of ash dancing in the evening sky, all those years ago. She thought of him every day and still missed him. She tried to think of all the happy times and not to dwell on her loss. It was hard.

The first year that they owned the Warren land they managed to complete the hedge reconstruction on half of the fields. It was in the second year that Tom, sitting up in his tractor ready to use the frontloader to move the woodpile into the flames, noticed how slow his mother had become, labouring over quite small branches and slowing down the procedure.

"Come on, Mother, speed it up. It'll be dark soon."

The previously spick and span farmhouse also showed signs of neglect, but it was when Florence climbed into the back of the Land Rover to strew hay to the cattle in the fields that autumn that Tom finally fully realised that she was struggling. He watched in his mirror as she tried again and again to lift the hay bale and balance it on the tailgate. Eventually she would do it, cut the binder twine and wearily throw the hay out to the impatient cows.

Tom, now worried, noticed she had developed a persistent cough and persuaded her to make an appointment with the surgery in the village. Her old family doctor had not seen her for years and was shocked by her appearance. He examined her carefully. He had heard how hard the death of William had hit her. His world was one of science, but really he thought she was dying of a broken heart. The whole village knew how close she and William had been.

"You are run-down both mentally and physically. I will prescribe a tonic but I would like you to take it easy and come back in three weeks."

The waiting room had been full of people sneezing and wheezing; maybe her cough developed into a chest infection picked up in the confined space. But she never saw the kind doctor again.

Tom found her dead two weeks later. She was curled up in her bed, looking like a tiny bag of bones, clutching a photograph of William to her chest. Tom prised it from her and saw his father looking back at him, love in his eyes. Without realising that this was an echo from the past, Tom muttered, "I never thanked her."

19

Tom missed his mother, moving slowly from kitchen to scullery to slow his rush to get back to the fields. She had always been there to listen to all his farming worries, had taken the long view, calming him when a crisis arose, lifting his spirits when things were bad. She had been such a constant unwavering force in his life, all those carefully prepared meals, his clean clothes always in a neat pile at the end of his bed, the socks folded in such a way that he could just put his toe in and then unfold them onto his foot with such ease. Now he desperately needed new farming equipment if he were to continue to farm alone. There had been a revolution in agricultural machinery that made it possible to do almost all the jobs himself. He could delay it no longer. He needed to make some very expensive purchases and to do so, he now realised, it was time to borrow from the bank.

After parking his old Land Rover in the square in Tavistock, a scrubbed-clean Tom crossed the road to the bank. He walked briskly in and found the manager ready to see him. In the soundproof inner office all was quiet and characterless; this was not a world Tom felt comfortable in. Thinking of the value of his acres, he had not expected any opposition to his request for a much larger overdraft, so he was shocked when the bank manager leafed through his carefully prepared business plan rather dismissively, pushed his chair back and said, "Sorry, Tom, but we just can't do that. Maybe twenty thousand pounds but certainly not the seventy you are asking for. You see, you need to be careful, Tom. Interest rates are on the rise and you do not want to be working just to pay the bank. Farming is facing a tough time. Sell a bit of land. That is what I suggest. I can do the twenty thousand but that is the limit."

He stood to indicate the end of the meeting, and shook Tom's hand. It was a very different Tom who walked out of the bank. His spirits drooped. His shoulders rounded, he climbed up into the driving seat and noticed, for the first time, stiffness in his knees.

When Tom got home he found a message from the bank manager.

"Tom, I have had an idea. Can you pop in to see me tomorrow? Ring me back when you pick up this message and we will fix a time."

The next day Tom was once more in the bank manager's office.

"Hello, Tom. I have just had a thought that might help you. Come in and sit down. There is to be a new area manager here and the one we have chosen wants to keep his house in Berkshire and rent a farmhouse near Tavistock. He wants to take a long lease and wants it unfurnished. Couldn't you move into that little cottage now that old Walter and Edna have retired. I think they have moved into sheltered housing, haven't they? It just might help this new chap and certainly the rent would be a big help with the cash flow?"

"Sounds too good to be true." Tom's spirits lifted.

"Get him to come and have a look. If it suits him I will move all the old furniture out and put it in the barn. If he likes it, let's hope he does, then I'll get my agent to contact you to set up the lease. Thanks a lot." It was a much happier Tom who drove home from Tavistock.

Even with this solution Tom decided he would take the manager's advice and sell the field. Then he would not need to borrow the twenty thousand. He knew interest rates were going higher and higher. The field up by the road, next to the village, should be easy to sell. The local agent thought he could get the best price at auction.

Back at Hawcoombe Tom wandered from room to room. He had not even entered the extra bedrooms since Florence had died. They smelled musty and damp. It would be good for him to have a clear out and he remembered Walter and Edna's cottage being warm and cosy. Tom felt happy and keen for this new step.

In six weeks' time they were gathered at The Bedford Hotel. Tom noticed at least five local farmers around the room, all making a good pretence of looking unconcerned. In a farmer's book it was a sin to get rid of land, and Tom felt guilty, as though he had let his family down. In front of his neighbours, who all lived by the same rule: 'Never sell land', he felt embarrassed.

There was total silence as the auctioneer picked up the gavel, introduced himself and described the well-fenced fifteen-acre field with access from the main road. Water came from a stream in the corner that had never been known to run dry.

I never said that, thought Tom; he had brought in an emergency water tank at least twice in the dry summers.

An old neighbour started the bidding at fifteen thousand; within a moment it climbed to eighteen and up in twos, bouncing from one farmer to the next. At thirty thousand, the bidding slowed.

The auctioneer tried to jolly them along. "Come on, gentlemen, this is excellent permanent pasture, and you can check your stock over the fence without getting out of your Land Rover."

What nobody had noticed was that a man in a dark grey suit had appeared in the doorway. He had a comfortable paunch, grey smartly cut hair and a well-groomed look of opulence. At thirty-one thousand, he raised his hand. The old farmers turned stiffly to see the opposition, their chairs scraping against the slate floor. The two remaining farmers dropped out and the field went to the stranger in the suit. Nobody knew him; everybody was curious.

Later, Tom, thrilled with the price, got a call from a Mr Rowlings. He explained that he was the agent for the purchaser of Tom's land. He then, very surprisingly, asked Tom if he would like to rent it back. The rent was much lower than the norm, and Tom accepted, but was left wondering what was up and felt in some way that he had been outmanoeuvred. He was not sure why.

20

Of late, Tom had become a bit of a ladies' man. He realised that he could charm girls with his chatter about his animals. They found his broad shoulders, kind grin and naive talk of simple country things a great relief after so many young men who worked for software companies and did not know how to change a tyre. Tom was competent, quiet, and made them feel feminine and protected.

They came and went, these girls. Some were nurses, some worked in shops, some were teachers. They all seemed much the same and none gave him the slightest heartache. He thought of them only in terms of how they could enhance his farming life or answer his sexual needs. He wanted a physically strong woman who would be compliant. That much he knew.

Tom was working on the baler. He sighed and leaned back for a moment, stretching his back and rolling his shoulders. How many harvests had he seen home? Since Florence's death the time from cutting to stowing away the bales seemed to have lengthened and dragged, becoming longer and more wearisome with each year. Now he approached this harvest with dread. It was the final stage, with the trailer lined up by the barn and every bale needing manhandling into place, which he dreaded. Not even the thought of all this winter fodder safely stored in good order could lift his spirits.

Sometimes he went to The Old Plough in the evening but he felt he did not quite fit in. He stood with the other farmers, trying to joke and laugh with them, but there was reserve and a slight awkwardness about him. Driving along the Devon lanes, he watched to see who cut the first field of silage and he judged them by the state of their stone hedges. Sitting in his Land Rover, he looked into their fields at their ploughing, comparing it unfavourably with his own. This negativity he could not acknowledge or recognise as loneliness. He just went on putting one foot in front of the other, unable to lift himself from his farming rut.

Book Two

1

A taxi swooped down to Paddington station. A young woman jumped out and paid her fare. She was tall and slim with shoulder-length red hair. She wore jeans and a smart green jacket, a red scarf knotted around her neck, and now she walked briskly towards the platforms. She knew where to go, for she had done this journey many times before. Her name was Freya Drummond and she was bound for Devon to visit her elderly mother, Bridget.

Freya found her train waiting and filling up fast. She ran along the platform, her suitcase on wheels clattering behind her. She hoped to find a window seat and a table, but she was out of luck. Parking her case, she squeezed into the only seat available, with her back to the engine. Opposite her, the dreaded combination of a mother and her hyperactive three-year-old sat among already opened crisp packets, colouring books and felt tips, taking up all the table space. Freya's thoughts of a peaceful journey and time to read her book faded. She felt trapped. But before they even left the suburbs she saw that the small boy opposite was, thankfully, looking sleepy. His head drooped and Freya opened her Hardy novel, occasionally glancing up to see the countryside unfurling. A man in a pinstriped suit next to her was engrossed in a copy of *The Times*, holding it like a barrier against humanity, and so he remained for the rest of the journey.

Sunlight glistened on the estuary of the Plym as the train braked for the approach to Plymouth. As it slowed for their arrival Freya rose to gather her belongings. With no time to pause, she grabbed her luggage and ran to platform three so as not to miss the connection for Bere Ferrers. The whistle blew and she climbed in and settled in her seat as they rumbled through suburbs, then into a deep rubbish-encrusted embankment and out again into sunlight. The little stations of St Budeaux, the Dockyard and Keyham had weeds creeping over the once-pristine platforms and undergrowth invading from each side of the line, buddleia and laurel fighting for light. On the left, Brunel's bridge, once the lowest span over the river, now had competition from the Tamar Bridge, teeming with traffic heading west to Cornwall. The river ran north, parallel to the railway. Freya watched from the window as six strong women, hauling on long oars, battled against the tide, their bright-coloured gig making fair progress and the cox shouting encouragement as they tilted back and forth. Crossing the Tavy Bridge, the little train reduced speed, and Freya began to collect her things. The sight of russet-coloured cows in lush green fields lifted her heart. She was home.

The platform at Bere Ferrers was deserted. She waited here for Reg, the unofficial taxi driver. He'd probably be late, so she wandered along the short platform. Pausing by a brass plaque, she read the names of the ten New Zealand soldiers who had died, yards from where she stood, run down by the express train heading at speed towards Plymouth. As she did so, Freya realised that today was the anniversary of their deaths, 24 September 1917. On this beautiful late summer's day, the leaves still clinging to the trees, and the birds singing, she felt sad.

Reg finally arrived and took Freya away from her thoughts of the young New Zealanders. His greeting was the same as it had always been. He used to pick her up when she came home from school and would inevitably say, "Hello, maid, my, you've grown. What have they been feeding you on?"

Today was no exception. Tucked into the front of his old Ford, Freya listened to the local gossip as they swung from the Tavy side of the peninsula to the Tamar – same old thing, trouble about planning permission and footpaths.

The tide was still running in fast, and as they passed Weir Quay, Freya saw the same gig being pulled up the slipway by the seven well-built girls, faces aglow, straining to slide the heavy boat up the beach.

"That is the new gig. Very popular but of course it is all the newcomers who are enjoying it, not the locals."

Freya felt it was best not to comment. Obviously parish politics were involved.

Finally, down the long drive, with only the occasional pothole, and home. The dogs barked, the door opened, and there her mother stood, her arms held out in welcome. This greeting too seemed to have been the same as long as Freya could remember. London already seemed a distant dream.

Mrs Bridget Davenport steadied herself against the

doorpost as she slipped on her old green boots to come out to welcome her only daughter.

It was comforting that Freya's mother always looked the same – an old quilted blue jacket, carefully patched and re-bound around the cuffs. Rather baggy rust-coloured corduroy trousers were hitched up by a belt from a long-dead mackintosh, and on her feet were her gumboots, endlessly dragged on and off as she moved from garden to kitchen. Her hands were those of a countrywoman who had no time for fripperies, wrinkled and sunburnt, and her face was unadorned save for a pat of powder before church. Everything was clean and an identical outfit would be lying in the drawer ready to replace the dirty one.

Freya came down to Devon from London every six weeks and was lulled into a false sense of security by the never-changing mother who had always made her feel so safe and secure.

To begin with, Freya noticed very little difference in her mother. Bundled up in warm clothes, her weight loss was not apparent. The tea was the same, although the inevitable Victoria sponge cake seemed to be lacking any raising agent. Of course, Freya made no comment but she noticed that, while she was given a large slice, her mother did not eat anything.

2

Bridget's friend, Albertine Kitto, called quite frequently and the two would sit chuckling about the old days. Freya got to know Albertine over this time. She was years younger than Bridget but older than Freya and she bridged the age gap. She had a smallholding further upriver. It was Albertine who had rung her to tell her of her mother's failing health.

The next few months were very precious for mother and daughter. The rushing about that they had been used to came to an end. Freya did the minimum to keep the house ticking over and through the winter months she battled to keep her mother warm. The older woman spent a lot of time sitting in the window, her knitting on her knees, but it never seemed to progress. If she heard Freya approaching she'd pick it up and sort out the four needles she always used. But Freya knew that it was abandoned the moment she walked out. There had never been the time over the years to learn the mysteries of this four-needled knitting or how to turn a heel on a handmade sock – never the right moment. This was only one of Freya's regrets, but then who wore handmade socks these days?

Eating was a problem for Bridget, but at least one large

bowl of porridge went down at breakfast, with salt of course and, surprisingly for one so self-denying, lots of double cream. It was on the morning that Freya's mother said in a quiet voice, "No porridge for me, darling," that Freya called Dr Johnson from the Bere Alston surgery. He had struck up a good rapport with his favourite patient over the years. Unbeknownst to Freya, he had been monitoring her mother's progress for a few weeks and knew of the cancer. He also knew that she totally accepted that this was the end. She wanted no surgery and no drugs. She was ninety-seven years old and had had a wonderful life, as she reassured Freya and Albertine. Her poor old knees that had given such good service for the first seventy years of her life were now worn out. She had struggled around with a stick, then with two; finally she had mastered crutches, but she could not accept the next stage, a wheelchair. Now, Dr Johnson came down the drive in his precious soft-top Morris Minor, full of kindness and knowledge.

Having made an examination, he returned to Freya in the kitchen.

"It won't be long, Freya. She is so peaceful. So accepting and quite ready for the end. I don't need to tell you how wonderful it is for me to have her as my patient. Can you manage, or would you like her to go into Tavistock hospital? They are very good there."

"We'll be fine, but thank you."

The next day, her mother did not get up. She lay in her bed, only occasionally turning her head to look out over a stormy Tamar. That night Freya slept in the little room next door with the baby alarm on. Her mother wanted to listen to the wireless.

All night long Freya popped in and out. Through the alarm she could hear her mother listening to the test match, as she had always done. In the early morning Freya heard her speak in the faintest whisper.

"England. Hopeless."

She meant the test match score, of course, and Freya laughed. Later that day her mother asked, "Freya, can you open the window? Now sit me up with lots of pillows." She winced with pain as Freya tried to haul her up, as gently as possible, but her bones grated audibly. The wind buffeted the curtains and swirled around the room.

"There, now I can feel the wind on my face. I'm ready to go."

It was as though her soul blew out into the fresh air.

Dr Johnson returned. Freya watched him gently taking her mother's dear emaciated old hand in his. She left them together.

When he left he said, "Are you all right, Freya? Do you want anybody with you?"

"I'm fine." She turned away, not wanting him to see her stricken face.

During the course of that day, Bridget slipped into a deep sleep from which she never awakened.

3

Her mother's cottage lay above a bend in the river, on a plateau, surrounded by woodland. It was a place of dreams. It had once been the Count House to a now totally derelict silver and lead mine. No trace of this was visible and ivy had covered everything in a mantle of green leaves. Looking south down the river, the cottage caught all the sun and nestled snugly into the hillside, avoiding almost every angle of wind.

Freya had been nearly grown up by the time her father died. After a distinguished army career he had retired with the family to farm near Chagford. He had been an old man then, twenty-five years older than his wife, so both Freya and her mother had done a great deal of the work. It had been a successful enterprise. After his death, Freya and her mother had sold up. Chagford had become a popular place, and they got a very good price for the farm. At the time, this little cottage overlooking the Tamar had been a lucky find despite being in bad repair. They had rented a house in the village while renovations were completed. Freya had been in her last year at school before going off to Durham University, so she had never really lived in the Count House as her home.

Now, she had to make some decisions. To begin with she

thought that she would sell up as soon as possible and go back to London to pick up the threads of her career. But things took time; probate seemed to take for ever and during this period she began to settle and enjoy country life again. It was March, and spring arrived suddenly in the valley. Her impatience to be gone, away from sad memories, receded. She watched long-tailed tits darting from tree to tree in their bouncing flight; there was a bright flash as a kingfisher sped by close to the bank. Two swallows perched on the telephone wire. Down on the shore, the geese chattered, and she soon became entranced by the tide's unending ebb and flow.

She did chat to a few neighbours; Albertine was very attentive and came often to sit in the kitchen to talk to Freya, telling her about her flock of sheep and her single-suckle herd of South Devon cattle. But mostly Freya kept to herself. It was her way and she was happy in her own company.

The cottage was full of bookshelves crammed with every sort of book. Having not had time in her busy adult life to read anything that was not part of her career, Freya now resolved to get through every novel and poetry book she had not previously read. It was an eye-opener for her. Her mother, who had made lots of pencil marks in the margins and underlined sections of text that she had particularly liked, had read each book. Much-loved volumes of poetry looked very thumb-marked and all her favourite verses were circled in pencil. There were gardening books, rows of them, great tomes of Edwardian wisdom. They looked daunting. One, more modern, caught Freya's eye: she read that in mild climates potatoes could be planted in March.

Pulling on her gumboots, Freya headed for the kitchen garden. There were six raised beds and all had been dug over the previous autumn and made ready for planting. Gravelled paths ran between each, and surrounding the entire garden was a picket fence and wire netting. Freya remembered how thrilled her mother had been; this was her first really rabbit-proof garden and she had loved it. Until a week before she died she had manoeuvred herself around on her crutches busily tidying up and, in her head, planning the planting for the next spring. Freya peered into the Victorian terracotta rhubarb forcers. They were works of art, beautiful shapes, with yellow lichen dusting the summits of their russet domes. She remembered them from Chagford days and how her mother had cherished them. Now, within, she saw the bright pink stalks of the young rhubarb contrasting perfectly with its acid green leaves.

In the old dilapidated potting shed, Freya found her mother's stainless steel spade. It had been a wedding present from her husband; one side was worn to a curve and holding it, Freya remembered her mother double-digging every bed, her old foot in galoshes on the lug of the spade. Freya decided she'd get going today and dig the trench ready for the seed potatoes. Tomorrow, she would drive into Tavistock to buy Sharp's Express; she remembered the variety.

The place had begun to work its magic, and Freya put off her return to London indefinitely. Soon after this, she went to visit Michael and Lucy, farming friends in Cornwall. After a good dinner, Michael said, "I've got something you might be interested in here. Come and have a look." They went out to the kennels and met a single fat collie puppy. Michael's very well-bred bitch had escaped five months earlier and he had not realised she was in pup; it was a great surprise to find her with a litter of six puppies when he had gone to collect her to do some sheep work one morning. There was just this one left and Michael was keen for her to go to a good home so he could get on with training the mother. Already called Meg by the children, she was only seven and a half weeks old. A twenty-pound note changed hands, and so started Freya's and Meg's many years of friendship. Meg, having had her last feed from her mother, curled up on Freya's knee and slept for the entire drive home.

Quite soon, as the puppy managed to lift her fat little body onto sturdy legs, Freya started walking her across the fields and teaching her basic manners. It was far too early, of course, but they both enjoyed it.

It was on one of these training trips that Freya became aware of the tenant farmer from the farm next door. He would always give her a cheery wave and a smile. But this time he stopped his Land Rover to admire the puppy; he got out and picked Meg up tenderly and let her cover his cheeks with licks. His name was Tom.

4

Freya grew daily to love not only the cottage but also the whole peninsula with its river boundaries keeping the rest of the world at bay.

For a little old lady whose greatest treat was cream on her porridge, Freya's mother had surprisingly left enough money for her daughter to manage financially. At least she had breathing space to decide on what direction her life should take. At the moment, well into spring, she was pretty determined to stay in Devon.

Beside the cottage were level plateaus and steep banks dropping to the river below, and there were two fields. Here her mother had kept Jacob sheep for their wool. However, for the last five years they had been rented on a year-on-year basis to Tom Northwood, the same tenant who farmed the neighbouring land. Lady Day was approaching and Freya wondered whether she should take the land back in hand. She knew this would tie her down but maybe that was what she needed: Meg, some sheep, and maybe a horse would all rely on her. She realised that she was missing being needed now that her mother had died. She thought about her life in London, the routine and, of course, her colleagues. At this stage, Freya did not allow herself even to start dwelling on the loss of her husband and the girls. She had determined to put her past behind her. She'd just build a new life, here among the fields of the valley.

Friday was market day in Tavistock. Freya rang the auctioneer and told him that she was looking for a few Jacob sheep.

"I've got the perfect thing for you. Old Phil Dawe is giving up his smallholding and going into a home. He's got two Jacob ewes. He'd like it if they went to you. They're used to a bit of spoiling, mind."

"That sounds perfect." Freya felt pleased.

"I'll be putting them through about ten-ish next Friday."

Standing by the ring later that week, Freya felt conspicuous hemmed in on either side by farmers. She realised that they were all in a sort of uniform and there was only one other woman among them, Albertine Kitto. She was dressed identically to the men, pale green muddy wellingtons, checked shirt, worn old fleece and, on top, an ancient waxed jacket. She had a wind-beaten face and the brown skin emphasised her remarkable pale blue eyes. Her wrinkles somehow gave her more character and were settled in smile lines. Freya noticed all the farmers' hands on the rail around the ring, sausagey red fingers, twice the size of other mortals' and roughened by the elements. Their faces too showed the hardship of their lives; however, here among their own kind, the atmosphere was jovial. For them this was a highlight of their often lonely lives, and they were enjoying the banter and general chat about farming. Many had come down from the moor, as this livestock market was the nearest for many miles. They had travelled here in matching, battered old Land Rovers towing cattleboxes.

Freya felt their stockmans' eyes resting on her, appraising her and, embarrassed, quickly passing on. She'd done her best, mind you – tied back the flaming red hair and put on an old, wide-brimmed felt hat. Her well-worn green duffle coat, however, failed to disguise her neat figure, and her boots were definitely a mistake, dark green Hunters with buckles at the side – gentry wellies.

Of course, Freya had been to market with her father in Chagford days, but she had been a child then and had known many of the local farmers. To them, she was the little red-headed maid with the fat Dartmoor pony, who bravely galloped over the moor at breakneck speed to keep up when they were all out hunting. Here, she was the new girl. Seeing her discomfort, Albertine came over to talk to her. She and Freya had become close over the last few months.

Phil's ewes had just come into the ring.

"What do you think of them, Albertine?"

"Well, they're in lamb, definitely. They'll follow you around like dogs. Phil spoiled them. For you, on your own, that'll be a good thing. They'd find it tough to join a flock."

The bidding started. A hawk-eyed dealer from upcountry was the only other bidder. The sheep were knocked down to Freya for eighty pounds for the pair. Queuing outside the market office to pay, she was joined by Tom, the tenant farmer from next door.

"I saw you'd just bought those Jacobs. Would you like me to take them home for you? I've got a half-empty cattlebox.

I can put my tups in the front compartment and your ladies can go in the back."

"Thank you, Tom. That'll save a lot of bother. Shall I meet you at the field?"

"No, no. It's no trouble. I'll just shove them through the gate."

She noticed his high cheekbones and long limbs, unusual for this part of the world, where most farmers were short, barrel-chested and looked as though they had come over with the Spanish Armada.

Freya thanked him and returned home, satisfied with her morning's purchase.

5

The river swelled towards high tide, and stifling heat hung over the valley.

Freya called to Meg, who bounded up. She'd take her for an evening walk and think things through. They set off down what had been an ancient Devon green lane, now tarmacked. With the passing of time, the narrow passage had sunk deeply below the field level and it changed its appearance with the seasons, as though donning new dresses. First, in the spring, the daffodils and narcissus that had escaped from the fields clung to the vertical sides of the hedges, bringing hope and promise to a wintry world; they were followed by primroses and stitchwort. Next came the purple outfit – foxgloves and campion, ragged robin and willowherb. And now, as the summer solstice approached, the foxgloves still reigned supreme, while at the top of the hedge, level with Freya's nose, the honeysuckle had twined upwards towards the light and she breathed in the subtle scent. Over the hedge she could see the river beyond, bounded by bright green fields. There was an eerie light; the heat of the day was now threatened by the banks of cloud building up above the hills to the west. Deep in thought, Freya now entered Tom's farmyard. Ahead of her was a scene of frantic activity. On the left, pulled by an ancient, rusty tractor, a fully loaded trailer sagged under the weight of a vast stack of bales. Straight ahead, another trailer, half full, was being unloaded onto an elevator that rattled and shook as it carried a procession of bales to the top of the barn. A young man was heaving and swinging the bales one after the other, working hard to keep up with the elevator as it travelled unceasingly upwards.

Freya realised instantly that out here, beyond her own world, a drama was being played out. These men were trying to save the hay. The thunderous heat of the departing day was a precursor to a storm. Any moment, huge drops of rain could fall on the naked bales. Wet on the outside and damp within, they would ferment and become mouldy and useless.

An older man appeared in the upper entrance of the barn at the top of the elevator. He smiled broadly and gave her a wave. It was Tom.

"Could you do with another pair of hands?" she shouted, above the din.

"Yes please, we've still got half a field to come in."

"I will just go and change and be back in a moment."

Freya headed back up the road.

Once home, she changed her clothes quickly. She remembered to take some old gloves to stop the binder twine cutting into her hands. After filling a large bottle with elderflower cordial, she put this, some mugs and a box of flapjacks in a basket and ran back down the hill towards the farm.

*

The elevator was still clanking but the trailer was now empty and the young man had disappeared. Freya could hear voices high up inside the barn. Threading the handle of the basket over her shoulder, she used both hands to climb the wall of tightly packed bales and found the whole harvest party sprawled around on top of the hay. It was dim and shady in here but heat rose from the newly stacked hay, exaggerating the sweetness of its smell. Light shone through the slatted walls of the barn and tiny particles of dust danced in each beam. Both the elevator boy and Tom were stripped to the waist, bits of dried grass sticking to their sweating bodies. An old man with a walrus moustache, huge heavy boots and a dreadful khaki-coloured string vest tucked into baggy army trousers was holding their attention. There was a timelessness to the scene and Freya, in her denim shorts and rather too tight shirt, felt like an intruder, their earth colours contrasting with her shades of blue.

They were drinking tepid water from plastic bottles.

"Good of you to help, Freya," said Tom. "They're heavy bales, mind."

"You look dressed for the beach and very nice too," the old man said in that strong local drawl that was music to Freya's ears.

She started to unpack the basket.

"Oh my, this gets better and better, maid." His heavily wrinkled, weather-beaten face beamed appreciatively.

She moved from one to the other with her offering, stooping to each like a priest among communicants. Luckily, the gloom within the barn made it impossible for the men to see her colour rise as she became increasingly aware of the missing button on her shirt and the amount of leg exposed.

The young man, Daniel, was nurturing a rather unsatisfactory crop of stubble; he had a smooth brown muscular body, almost hairless. Sitting between him and Bill, the old man, Freya was disturbed by the overwhelming smell of male bodies and edged further away.

"That was good of you, Freya. Just what we needed. It's a real scorcher. Six now and as hot as it was at noon," Tom said. "Come on, lads, let's get going. Bill, you work the elevator and, Daniel, you look as though you need to get out of the sun for a while – you stack bales in here."

He rose and swung down out of sight, but in a trice reappeared, driving a different tractor pulling a very rickety trailer that was already fully loaded. He lined it up next to the elevator.

"Freya, you come with me. We'll get the next load." He was back in the driving seat of the rusty tractor and holding open the door. Pulling herself up, she was delighted to find a comfortable little perch just behind Tom in the corner of the cab. The engine vibrated and shook as they navigated their way around other machinery, out through the gate and across a rutted field to an opening in the hedge. Beyond this was the hay field.

Alone in the cab with Tom, Freya suddenly felt shy and tongue-tied. The roar of the engine luckily made speech unnecessary anyway. Sitting slightly behind Tom, she could study him unnoticed. First, she watched his hands on the steering wheel. They were deeply sunburnt, broad and capable. As he changed gear she noticed, with surprise, the beautifully shaped nails that had obviously been well cared for, cuticles pushed back and clear pale half-moons contrasting with the deep colour of his skin. Nice hands, thought Freya.

Just as she was studying the way the hairs grew on his forearm, the tractor came to a juddering halt. They were at the brow of a field with land running south to the Tamar. The river had snaked around and also marked the northern boundary. This lozenge-shaped piece of land was surrounded by water on all sides except for a narrow neck to the east. The tide now fully up, boats rested peacefully on their moorings. The river shimmered. Cattle were grazing in deep clover on flat land reclaimed from the estuary and protected by a sea wall. The low evening light accentuated the contrast between their deep bracken-coloured coats and the greenness of the grass. Each cow had a calf at foot. They all looked identical to Freya.

Yet another tractor with a 'flat eight' behind was parked on the stubble. Freya had seen this in action before and knew that it was used to collect eight bales at a time, squeeze them tightly together, and then carry them to their destination.

"You climb up on the trailer and I will bring over each load." Tom looked at her questioningly to see if she understood how this was going to work, not wanting to tell her something she already knew.

"Each time you will have to manoeuvre things around to make a good load. Tell me if you get tired." So Tom came across with the bales and Freya rearranged them to fit snugly. Every third time, she climbed up a layer. She was determined not to show weakness and worked systematically, thinking hard how to conserve her energy. It was going to be a long evening.

On top of the bales, Freya worked on. Thank goodness she had become strong and fit while working to reclaim the neglected land around her mother's house.

When they reached what Freya thought must be the top layer, she paused briefly to look around her. A scowling bank of grey cloud was coming in rapidly from the west. It looked angry and threatening. Occasionally, groups of shelduck flew raggedly upstream, the white of their plumage looking almost translucent. The river was blue-black now and the boats, cattle and fields had taken on an unnatural radiance in the strange light. Above her, Freya could hear a lark singing.

Finally, the load was considered complete and Tom gave her a thumbs-up sign. She was a little concerned as to how she was going to get down; peering over the edge, she saw that he had raised the grab, which looked like a great square claw, and now it formed a bridge between her and his tractor. Oh God, she thought, does he really expect me to clamber down that? It was the crossover from hay trailer to the claw that worried her. Once, a long time ago, she had become immobile with terror on a steep scree slope on Snowdon; her body had hugged the slope and her legs had been spread out, refusing to move. A fear of heights had stayed with her.

Tom smiled encouragingly and waited. She left the seeming security of 'her' trailer and climbed down, every step taken with great care. The last bit was a six-foot jump. Tom, out of his cab now and on the ground, was waiting to catch her. She leaned forward, reached for his outstretched hands and jumped. His hands felt warm and dry, with extraordinary hardened palms. Not the sort of hands that usually came into contact with Freya's. In her nervousness, she laughed.

They repeated this procedure four times, filling trailers, taking them to the elevator and then back to the field for another load.

Each time, Freya's confidence in her high-level antics grew. Tom's encouraging smile for the last jump seemed to gain importance. She looked forward to the brief contact with those hands.

A few bales were left in the field as they made their final trip back to the yard. As she bounced along on her perch next to Tom, the wheel hit a stone and she lurched into him. Her softness seemed to merge with his firm bulk.

"Sorry." She levered herself upright. He smelled so good. Not like the acrid smell of the men in the barn, but a sweetness she could not define. Was the intense atmosphere between them of her own imagining? The sky darkened. Far away in the direction of Cornwall, there was a deep-throated rumble of thunder.

Tom parked the last laden tractor in the empty cattle shed beside the hay barn.

"Too dark for you chaps in there. Let's call it a day. I'll square you up Friday. Well done. I'll just go and stack up those last few bales. You go on home, and thank you."

"You've had some good help, boss. The maid speeded everything up, and we've enjoyed her pretty smile, and that elderflower cordial came at just the right moment." Daniel helped the older man lift his bike into the battered pick-up. They left noisily; the silencer had seen better days. A cloud of dust soon obscured the hands waving out of the windows as they roared off. Freya stood in the yard, a little uncertain.

"I'll give you a lift up the lane in a moment, but first I've got to tidy up those last bales. Do you want to come?" Freya was relieved to stretch out her time with him and instantly agreed.

*

They travelled out to the field for the last trip and, working by headlights, they gathered the bales together and made castles of them so that the inevitable rain would spoil only the outside ones. The humidity now felt so high that Freya could almost sense the huge drops of water that would fall on her warm skin.

Finally, all was finished. Back in the yard, Tom handed back Freya's basket and she poured him some cordial. With surprise, she noticed that as he took the beaker his hand shook so much that he nearly spilled the drink. Almost involuntarily, as if to a child, she steadied his hand with both of her own. She glanced quickly up and their eyes met and held for an extra second. The darkness wrapped around them. It was with difficulty, as though pulling against the magnetism of opposite poles, that they regained composure.

At the top of the drive, Freya jumped out. There was now awkwardness between them. Nothing had been said. After thanking her for her help rather formally, Tom drove off quickly. If he gave her a wave, she did not see it, as it was now quite dark.

Home and upstairs, Freya ran her bath. Standing by the window, waiting for the tub to fill, she watched downstream where road and river converged. The lights of a fast-moving vehicle pierced the gloom and then the backlights as it receded into the distance, rounded the corner and was gone.

Climbing into the bath, her legs stung. From where her shorts had ended to her ankles were thousands of tiny scratches. Freya had been oblivious to these as she battled with the bales. Just before she lowered herself into the water, she heard the first heavy drops of rain.

6

A newly washed dawn greeted Tom when he woke. The fields glistened in the early-morning sun. It was as though the earth was sighing with relief after the weeks of drought. Tom's feet hit the floor at a run. He felt full of energy and, looking out of the window, he was, at last, proud of his beautiful acres, his well-trimmed hedges and, just beyond the gate, his herd of South Devon cattle. Their coats gleamed in the sunshine – just like Freya's hair, he thought, remembering in more detail the previous evening. He rushed through his stock check, pausing only briefly to give Beth a scratch, and then, jumping into his Land Rover, he headed for his rented land where a few bales of hay still lay in the field, drying out.

Tom's days usually started with an unattainable list of chores in his head. He never achieved them all and would climb into his rather gritty bed at the end of the day feeling disappointed at his lack of progress. But this morning he felt good about his farming, not an emotion he was used to. He drove past the track leading to Freya's cottage, slowing in case she appeared. Had he imagined it all? Nothing had been said.

First, he drove out to the hay field and spread the castled bales out to dry in the sun. All day, as he checked gate-hangings, mended bits of fence, looked with pleasure at the fast-growing lambs, his eyes inevitably travelled back to Freya's track, and he tried to imagine what her day's routine would be, only to realise that he really had no idea. Around three in the afternoon, he went to the tool shed and looked out his father's old viskie – not many people still called it that. It was a perfect mattock for digging up the roots of docks or thistles. He slung it over his shoulder and went off to the big field between Freya's cottage and her sheep paddocks. He started to walk around the perimeter where the steep slopes on the field margins below the stone hedges did not allow the tractor and topper to reach. Opportunist thistles had established themselves, so he swung the pick-like viskie and, with perfect aim, dug them and their roots up. Each time he swung, his eyes swept the horizon for sight of the redhead and the little puppy. He was halfway around before he saw her; a whole field's length lay between them. He shouldered the viskie and, suddenly, as he walked towards her, he felt embarrassed and tongue-tied. How should he greet her? She was out of his league.

Absolutely nothing had happened, Freya reassured herself. But the world she woke up to was quite different too. Where there had before been a rather bland contentment to her life, the moment she opened her eyes this morning, Freya felt her heart pounding. Tom, the shape of him, his smell, his voice, the touch of those hands on hers…but surely it had meant nothing. She must pull herself together and get on with her day. She was not a teenager; she'd had a husband, lovers, and her logical mind had made a decision about the course of her life, hadn't it? She had

155

had enough of the turmoil love affairs can bring and had been determined to steer a steady course in the direction she now wanted her life to go.

Turning to the window, she immediately looked downstream to where she had seen the lights of the Land Rover disappearing the night before. Nothing.

She dressed with more care than usual and paused to apply some mascara. What on earth was she doing? Making the bed, she noticed tiny bits of hay from her hair scattered on the pillow, and almost as if to remind herself that last night had actually happened, Freya looked down at her bare legs and saw the crisscross of scratches.

The day passed in a sort of dream. She could not settle. Even Meg's antics did not hold her attention. Freya made herself eat an apple and cheese for lunch, but she did not feel at all hungry. By mid-afternoon she reasoned with herself that she should visit the sheep, and so set off with Meg at her heels. They did a little training but both soon wearied of that.

She looked across the field and there was Tom. His tall, slim figure, long-legged and agile, was silhouetted against the afternoon sky. Just at that moment, he glanced up, the viskie now rested on his shoulder as he turned to walk towards her. For both of them this seemed a great distance, hanging in time. Neither heard the lark above.

7

There are no words to say how, quite suddenly, two people can fall in love; it cannot be explained. It is like an illness. For both Tom and Freya, it simply happened. Of course, neither could see that they were both coming from a past of great loneliness and overwhelming loss. Was this just a physical passion?

That wonderful golden summer would be etched in their memories for ever. The sun seemed to shine every day. At high tide, they swam in the river. Tom had never thought of doing this before. Freya would take picnic lunches to the fields and, before long, was up on the tractor helping with rolling the grass and watching the straight lines of green stretching behind her like a wake. In the dust on the dashboard, Tom would write instructions about the gears. Freya loved the Fergie's pictures of a hare for 'fast' and a tortoise for 'slow'. Internationally recognisable!

Almost all their meals were eaten outside. They took Freya's camping gas out to the west-facing field and cooked sausages as the sun dropped below the horizon. At midsummer, they timed the sun's departure after yet another perfect day; it was nearly ten o'clock. The afterglow of the sunset was reflected in the river and lengthened their evenings still further.

Freya did try to point out that they had certain cultural difficulties, to which Tom replied, laughing, "You may have cultural difficulties, I have only agricultural difficulties!" He was funny and unique and unspoiled and kind and practical and…Freya could have gone on for ever. She adored him and, in those sun-drenched days, he could do no wrong.

Secretly at first, Tom would visit Freya in the evenings and, inevitably, would leave in the early dawn. He travelled on an ancient motorbike, which he hid discreetly in the hedge nearby. Freya cooked exotic and delicious meals. They fell into a routine without any discussion of how their relationship would unfold. Day by day, their lives became entangled.

Freya was thirsty for knowledge about agriculture. She learned quickly and applied her passion and curiosity to a way of life that was set in stone and very traditional. She quickly grew to love Tom's farm, and especially his beautiful cows, learning to talk gently to them and scratch them at the base of their tails. They would stand, mesmerised.

Tom and Freya lived totally in the present, like children. It was as though both were afraid of discussing anything beyond the next week, as though they were holding their breath, the present too precious even to hope for a future. Slowly, Tom's clothes took up a chest of drawers in Freya's house, then a wardrobe. Dirty farm overalls piled up in front of her washing machine. She spent every moment she could helping him. It was easier just to get on with what was in front of them rather than to look at the big picture.

Freya felt physically sick with love and both she and Tom lost a stone in weight. This feeling of nausea she attributed to emotional upset. She had felt this after the death of Christopher and the girls – a physical and constant sickness. She was surprised that this could be caused by extreme joy as well as extreme distress, and wondered in which 'tiny ivory cell' the difference lay.

That Tom was happiest on the farm became obvious to Freya, so their days were spent working together doing whatever seasonal tasks presented themselves. At the end of August, Tom got out the green combine harvester, greased and cleaned it and prayed that this ancient machine would just do one more season. He made the same prayer every corn harvest, and on and on went the same dear old combine. It was the only one Freya had ever seen which had no cab. Tom would sit perched up in the open, dust blowing all around him, the sun beating down. He'd be there for hours, his brow furrowed as he concentrated hard, looking down at the header as it moved through the corn. Freya was horrified at his burnt skin and tried to get him to wear sunglasses and put on sun cream. He wouldn't. He took no care of his body; it was as though he were punishing himself. Freya did not like vain men who worried endlessly about clothes and ailments, but this was ridiculous, and she did her best to look after him. She rode around the fields with him; it was noisy, dusty and uncomfortable. She felt more useful driving the tractor and trailers and quickly learned to reverse the load into the shed and empty the grain out into the pit ready to be sent by elevator to the bins. It was not easy and Freya had to concentrate hard to get the trailer to just the right position. With a swoosh the grain would cascade down into the pit. As the dew started to fall, their day would end and back they would go to cook a meal. When Tom got home, he would usually have a headache from being too long in the sun. Looking at the field of stubble, Freya would feel a huge satisfaction in their achievements. They would eat mechanically before falling into an exhausted sleep.

With the grain safely in the bins and the straw baled up, the farming year was meant to take a breath. Knowing this, Freya once managed to pack a picnic supper and, with much grumbling and resistance from Tom, after a full day's work they drove to the coast. She took him to her favourite little valley where North Devon cattle grazed beside a turbulent sea. Here, she pointed out the ruins of a waterwheel that had milled corn. Dropping down through the fields of the valley, she showed him the old green lane where copper from the mine on the cliffs had been pulled up. In Freya's head, she was back in the nineteenth century; she could visualise the horses straining between the shafts as they hauled the ore up the valley. Tom, on the other hand, was staring at the dark brown cattle, comparing them unfavourably with his own South Devons.

"Too fat. They're always too fat."

They climbed up steep age-old steps to the top of the cliffs, and Freya unravelled the picnic treats. Immediately, they were surrounded by flying ants, which got inside the wine bottle, settled on the quiche and bothered them both. Tom, totally distracted, got up and prepared to leave. Freya's eyes were on the horizon and the little boats far out to sea. She thought she could make out Lundy Island, but perhaps it was only a container ship heading for the Bristol Channel.

*

A few days later Freya took lunch out to the field where Tom was collecting up the big bales with the tractor. Rusty, as it was called, whizzed about with a big spiked jaw for squeezing and grabbing the round bales and carrying them to be stacked on the trailer. Tom was so pleased to see Freya with her basket and rug and leapt from the cab to greet her. All around them the valley opened up, and on this day was overwhelmingly beautiful. Cows grazed in green fields next to golden stubble; above them was the bluest of skies and, high up, they could just make out a tiny lark, singing for all it was worth.

Tom looked at Freya in her skimpy sundress and felt a great wave of passion. She returned the look, desire for him in her eyes. They glanced around; the field was in full view of both the Devon and the Cornish sides of the valley. Later, they were not sure who had had the idea, and they teased each other about it. Tom jumped back into Rusty and started moving bales into a circle around Freya. In no time she had a very private house! Tom leapt inside and they fell into each other's arms, tearing off their clothes. If the stubble cut into her back, she was quite oblivious to it. When later the next crop was grown in that field, Tom said, "See how well it grows just there, Freya." She blushed and smiled.

8

The beautiful summer turned into a long autumn, full of late sunshine; they became, if possible, even closer. Their happiness seemed to radiate out to all those around them.

Tom thought he was in a dream. He had never felt like this before. Slowly the rumours had spread and his farming friends joked with him about his very evident weight loss.

"You'm like one of my tups when I take 'um out after the mating season." "If you don't look out, you'll fade away." But they liked to see Tom so happy and were more than a little curious about this unusual match.

Freya was now golden brown, being one of those redheads blessed with skin that tans easily rather than becoming freckled and pink. Tom watched her undress in the candlelight. If he had imagined the perfect woman, Freya would definitely be it. He knew that she had had two children; he'd seen the photographs, but something made him hesitate and he asked no questions about her former life. She'd tell him when she felt the time was right. He lay with his hands linked behind his head and just watched her, that mane of dark red hair swinging forward, and he longed for the next step and to feel her skin next to his… He felt lucky.

*

The first job on these early autumn mornings was to take the hay out to the cattle still grazing in the fields with their now quite large calves. The two of them would heave five or six bales into the back of the Land Rover and set off, amid diesel fumes. The cattle, recognising the engine noise, would come bowling across the field towards them, calling intermittently. Freya would hop out, get into the back of the Land Rover, climb on top of the heap with a knife, cut the baler twine and fling sections of hay to the hungry animals, distributing it far and wide. So enthusiastic were the cows that they would put their wet shiny noses right up next to Freya and sometimes amble off with a thatch of hay balanced on their huge horns – she loved that and would laugh out loud. Soon, Tom told her, they would have to separate off the bull calves in case they served their sisters or mothers. The best heifer calves would be left with their mothers and would be given creep feed in the sheds during the winter and kept to increase the herd numbers. The second pick would be out-wintered on turnips, and the best of those sold to other breeders. Finally, those remaining were for slaughter.

One darkening afternoon Tom was sitting on a bale with Freya beside him, both sipping mugs of tea. Once again she noticed his hands shaking. His voice remained calm as he told her that in the late autumn of 1990 he had run short of cake for two rather thin-looking heifers. He had driven into Tavistock and bought the only couple of sacks of cattle feed they had in stock.

"They're really meant for dairy cattle but I don't see it will make much difference," the assistant had said. Unwittingly,

Tom had fed this concentrated feed to his cows. It was part of this consignment of feed that later the scientists had condemned as possibly contaminated and therefore a cause of the BSE epidemic, mostly affecting dairy cattle. As a precaution the government traced all the farmers who had bought part of this batch. It was enormously bad luck that Tom had bought the two sacks.

"Oh, Tom, how terrible."

"The cows were slaughtered and all their cohorts. I got good compensation but that's not the point. All these clever scientists and businessmen. They think they know it all. Just interested in how to make the most money, cutting corners; they even lowered the temperature at which they boiled the offal. Anyway no sensible person would dream of feeding the offal of infected sheep to live healthy cows."

He dropped his head into his hands.

"I really can't talk about it. It knocked the beef industry for six. Now I am clear of all that and I can start direct marketing to the public, but it was all a nightmare." Tom sat up and turned towards Freya.

"We can do this together – it will be a joint venture. Let's get started as soon as possible."

Tom scrambled to his feet and pulled Freya towards him, giving her a lingering hug.

Winter crept nearer, and at the end of September the rams were put in with the ewes. As they fitted the raddles, Tom explained to Freya how this worked. Each ram would have a leather harness with a coloured marker fitted onto the front; this would stain the backs of each ewe that had been served by the ram. The colours would be changed every three weeks, from red to blue, so that they would know that all the red-marked sheep would be the first to lamb and then the blue and finally the green. There would always be a few ewes left with no telltale mark on their backs; these would be left in with the rams in the hope that they would cycle with the next batch. If they still showed no marking when the last rams finally came out, then they would be considered barren and sold for meat. When the ewes grew near to their due dates, they would be moved into the sheds in order of priority, red, blue and finally green. Freya listened carefully, although she knew all this. At Chagford she and her father had run a tiny flock and only one colour had been needed. She remembered the old stone barn and the wonderful feeling of family unity during lambing. With Tom, it was all on a much bigger scale and much more serious.

There was a particular image that stood out strongly from that earlier time with her parents. It must have been during the Easter holidays; her father had rigged up a CCTV camera so that from his bed he could see the flock in the barn. He had loved the technology and was proud of this innovation in the ancient farm building. On that particular morning, he had seen five ewes in labour and had wakened Freya. Her mother was already up and had boiled the kettle. Knowing their tasks well, they had chatted and laughed, and had settled the new arrivals into their pens, deep in straw. Then they had left them, the sound of the ewes calling to their lambs still audible as they crossed the yard, their arms loosely linked. A thin dawn drizzle had made gentle halos around their hair and Freya remembered that special bleat of love when she had held her own baby girls years later. Somehow, this memory had stayed with Freya almost as though she were looking at a photograph.

They were dealing with the rams' feet before they put them in with the ewes. The ram felt Freya's grip on him loosening and suddenly made a bid for freedom.

"Oy, stop dreaming, maid, if we lose him we'll have to bring them all in again."

Must concentrate, thought Freya.

Of course, for the first year she saw the whole round of the seasons from a farmer's perspective; it was totally fascinating, and Freya was so keen to learn. Subsequently, when they were in the middle of a very repetitive chore, she would let her mind float away. She'd look up into the blue sky and would see a tiny aeroplane and imagine its destination; Tom would have to bring her back to reality with a shout.

Tom and Freya met Philip at a farm sale in the neighbouring parish; they had all been looking, with great interest, at an ancient threshing machine. Philip had started talking to Tom. Recently retired from farming, he had come to live in a cottage nearby. He was finding the change of pace difficult and instantly got into conversation with Tom about the state of agriculture. You could tell he was delighted to be discussing a subject that he felt so passionate about. As he left the field, he called over his shoulder, "If you want a hand with anything, let me know."

So it started. Philip became invaluable. He appeared before breakfast. During the next harvest he brought in the grain trailers and became a firm friend to both Tom and Freya.

Harvest over, when the winter arrived he was still keen to help and to be involved with every aspect of the farm. He worked hard and they all enjoyed supper around the kitchen table, making plans and reminiscing about the past. Philip really appreciated being fed and the company of both Freya and Tom made him feel less lonely, and he liked being needed.

Feeding cattle in the sheds every morning was a favourite job for Freya. She'd climb up the steep wall of straw, throw five straw bales down to Tom, then move to an area of hay, cut the string and throw it as accurately as possible into the racks below. After a week or two, she was an expert climber. Tom was impressed. Returning to ground level, together they would spread straw to make a good bed for the cows. Moving about between the animals, even on the coldest mornings they would be warmed up by their hot breath rising like steam around them.

When Philip was not with them, Tom and Freya would have comfortable evenings together. It was cosy in Freya's candlelit kitchen and Tom, being left-handed, would sit so his right hand could rest in Freya's left as they forked their food. Nights were the icing on the cake; their bodies fitted so well together and they both felt peaceful and happy. Like all people in love, they felt they were special.

Meg was becoming a useful member of the team. She soon learned to creep around the sheep and bring them back to either of her masters. Lying close to the ground, she'd guard a gateway and save a great deal of running. Secretly, as long as he thought no one would notice, Tom would praise her and, picking her up, would make much of her. She was easy to love and in the kitchen the almost full-grown sheepdog would sit on Freya's knee in the evenings, looking very pleased with herself!

"Not farmery behaviour," Tom said, remembering his previous sheepdogs with their matted fur tied up outside on a chain, with a barrel as a kennel. Freya simply smiled.

Tom surveyed his herd of cattle from the Land Rover, and wondered if he should enter the herd competition. He had never felt in a position to do this before but now, looking at them, he realised that they had never looked so good and he felt the moment had come. The competition had several classes, each one giving points towards the best herd, and Tom was becoming very proud of what he had achieved through his years of following his own criteria on conformation, hardiness and milk production. He ruthlessly got rid of any animals that did not fit his rules. Now, he thought, they were uniformly beautiful. He would try his luck. He went through the entry form with great care, muttering a little about the fee. The judges would arrive on the farm in September, so they planned which groups of cattle would be entered for the different classes. Certainly the bull had a very good chance, and the group of five heifers also pleased Tom; he felt excited and hopeful.

Freya knew that much was expected of her on the judging day on the refreshment front. The three judges would be with them by teatime, so she made scones, a sponge cake, chocolate brownies and shortbread. At each place the judges stopped, they would be plied with food. It was a very necessary part of the proceedings and Freya was aware that her role was important to Tom. After the men had walked around the different categories of cattle, they all arrived in Freya's kitchen, and she watched with amazement as they ate scone after scone followed by cake, brownies and shortbread, all washed down with strong sweet tea. She dreaded to think what their cholesterol count was!

"I told you they would eat lots," whispered Tom, while they waved to the rotund and jovial judges as they finally disappeared in a beautifully kept old Mercedes.

Six weeks later, Tom went to the AGM of the Cattle Breeders Club; he rang Freya on his way home.

"I got best bull and best collection of heifers, third in the cow class and first overall."

He was elated. This was the culmination of the years of thought that had gone into the breeding programme, not only in Tom's generation, but in his father's and in his grandfather's.

Freya put a bottle of champagne in the fridge and they sat in bed drinking it and celebrating the success of the herd.

It did not seem much of a prize to Freya when they had to host a herd visit and feed the forty farmers who wanted to see Tom's farm. Lunch was laid out on long tables and, once again, Freya was amazed by the huge quantities of food that disappeared. She did make one big mistake: no one touched the rice salad.

"They think it is foreign muck," Tom explained as Freya scraped the piles of rice into the hen bin.

"I wish you'd told me that before."

Lambing became a big date in the calendar. The rams having gone in with the ewes at the end of September meant the lambs were due at the end of February. Towards Christmas, the vet would come and scan each ewe to see how many lambs she was carrying. The ewes would then be put in different fields and fed according to whether they were carrying singles, twins or triplets. Fed too little and the lambs would not be viable, fed too much and the ewes with twins or triplets might get 'twin lamb disease' and there would not be enough nutrients passing to the embryos. Freya's father had farmed before all this high-tech scanning equipment had been invented, so it was an eye-opener to her and seemed a wonderful, if pricey, help to the shepherds. What with the marks on the sheep's backs to tell which date they were due and then more marks to show how many lambs they would have, the ewes began to look quite colourful.

Towards the end of February the floor in the barn was scraped clean by dear old Rusty the tractor, then thickly sprinkled with lime to cut down the risk of disease, and covered in a thick layer of straw.

"Same straw that built our secret house, Tom."

"Multipurpose, this straw." He winked at Freya.

Once the maternity wing was ready, all the sheep that were having twins and had red marks on their backs came inside. These were then fed and watched carefully for the first sign of lambing.

After supper, Tom would doze on the sofa. Freya would head for an early bed. Tom would get up between midnight and two to check the sheep. The alarm would ring at five thirty, and Freya would go to the lambing shed to see if anything had happened. Once a ewe had lambed, she and her babies would be moved into a private pen. Iodine would be sprayed on the lamb's navel to prevent infection, and the little family left to bond. Freya would feed up all the sheep inside and then head to the other groups in the fields on the quad bike loaded with sacks of sheep nuts and hay to refill the racks. Tom, after feeding the cattle, would join her and, together, they would take ewes with strong lambs out of the little pens to yet another field, which became the nursery. Each ewe would have a number on her side corresponding to the number on the lamb so that out in the field, Tom and Freya could recognise if any lambs had strayed from their mothers.

On those mornings, Freya, who loathed getting out of bed early, would feel the cold air on her face and see the mist rising off the river. Slowly, she would begin to feel better. Out there in the dawn, she knew that this was a special moment to treasure; she could see shelduck, egrets, herons and lapwings and hear the bleat of lambs and the haunting cry of a curlew; the first rays of sun would pierce the morning haze. This helped her to ignore the other mornings, when there was a biting cold wind, sleet, drizzle, and she had freezing hands, and to forget the orphans she had battled to feed and then found dead and the awful births ending in the death of not only the lambs, but also the dear old ewe. It was a hard time but in the years that followed, Freya remembered it with nostalgia and longing.

Tom took it all in his stride and seemed impervious to life and death. He just carried on, never for a moment pausing to wonder if anything could be done to ease the workload, to change the system or to take on more modern methods. His father had done it this way, so that would do for him. If he noticed how hard Freya worked, he certainly did not mention it.

9

Wearily, year after year, they would finally get to the end of lambing the main flock. But then, when they were thoroughly exhausted, it was the turn of the young sheep to lamb, and there was a second burst of activity. These year-old ewes, hardly more than lambs themselves, had been put in with the rams last, so that they would have more time to mature before lambing. They were difficult, and wild, as they were not used to being handled. They had started the lambing in February; it was now April, and Tom and Freya still had a large pen of orphans to bottle-feed three or four times a day, troughs to be filled and hay to go out to the fields. On top of that, the first calves were due.

Freya, having spent time many years before helping a cousin with a flock of two thousand sheep up north, had lots of ideas for greater efficiency, but she had learned to keep quiet. Tom would not change a thing.

At last, by the middle of April, it was time for the cows to be let out of their winter quarters and onto the fields. This was a great moment; off they would go, careering about, leaping, ducking and diving in a very un-cowlike manner! They would have mock fights with each other and, plainly, were very pleased to get out in the fresh air with their feet in the grass.

Checking them each day, Tom would look for the signs of calving, and Freya would scratch their backs, pulling out handfuls of their old winter coats. Mostly, the cows calved unaided, but as the years went by, more and more seemed to need assistance, and Tom would get out his calving machine, a great long metal pole with a winch on it, which, to Freya, looked like an instrument of torture; she shuddered at the sight of it.

Interrupted nights in the fields waiting for a birth punctuated the next few weeks for them both. They would find a cow off on her own, looking restless, with a full udder. She would hold her tail high and Tom would predict, usually with amazing precision, the time of her calving. Inevitably, it seemed to Freya, this happened between midnight and five in the morning. One late evening, they were watching the old cow called Beth as she swung her head towards her tail.

"She'll be an hour yet," Tom said, as he tried to drive the midges away from his face. Freya was covered in oil of citronella but, as usual, Tom had not put any on.

"Damn the little blighters, let's wait in the Land Rover." Sitting together in the quiet dark of the cab, they dozed; half an hour passed, then an hour. Just after midnight Freya peered at Tom's new watch, her birthday present to him. It showed the date, the nineteenth of May.

"Today would have been Alice's eighteenth birthday," she whispered.

Tom waited and stretched out his hand for hers.

"I'm sorry I have not been able to tell you, Tom. I just find

173

it easier to lock all that sadness away. But it is part of me and you should know."

"Tell me whenever you are ready, poppet," he said, giving her hand a gentle squeeze.

Sitting there, with the darkness around them, the occasional plover calling, and the muffled movement of the cows, Freya began her story.

"You know we lived in London, and I was doing my doctorate as well as my job."

She felt the guilt again, and moved swiftly on.

"We were all going to go skiing in Meribel. The children were so excited – they had never been before. I was feeling frantic. I was so behind. We decided that it was best all round if Christopher went with the girls and I got on with my work in peace. I had a deadline to meet.

"They were disappointed but, in a way, it was a treat to have their daddy to themselves. They did not see that much of him as he worked very long hours. He was a hospital doctor, but I've told you that."

Holding her hand, Tom could feel her pulse racing. He glanced quickly at his cow; she seemed to have gone off the whole idea and was lying down peacefully chewing the cud.

"They were to drive out there, so the hall was full of clutter, food for the journey, ski clothes, snow chains. We piled it all into the Volvo. Finally, they were ready, late as usual, and off they went to catch the ferry. Lots of goodbyes, and I remember first Emma, then Alice, leaning far out of the back windows as they rounded the corner and shouting at the tops of their voices, 'We love you, Mummy, see you in a week.' They were so happy. The awful thing is that, when I closed the front door, I leaned against it and wallowed in the silence and rushed straight upstairs to my little office to start work."

The cow gave a strangled moan; they looked up and saw her heaving in the middle of the last contraction.

"Sorry, sweetheart, must go." Freya felt frustrated as she had been on the brink of telling her whole story. But now she had to seal it in. She followed him and held the torch. Before they reached the cow, Beth had produced a steaming wet bull calf all on her own. Tom sprayed the navel with iodine; Freya cleared mucus from its mouth and they retreated to the Land Rover. Within five minutes, the calf was up on its feet and had found its mother's udder.

"A lovely strong little calf. Come on, Freya, let's get back to bed." Tom was asleep before Freya had finished brushing her teeth.

In the next few days there seemed no opportunity for her to continue to tell him about her family. She felt that he did not want to know. Once again she was sealing in the story.

Tom worked out that Freya had been talking about something that had happened a dozen or so years ago.

Best left, he thought. He had followed this path all his life and felt it was the right one.

In among the routine of farming there were, of course, dramas.

10

After days of heavy rain, the field beside the river flooded and the water of the estuary surged in over the top of the sea wall. The rams, which had been grazing there, moved to the tussocks of fresh grass on the very edge of the river.

Tom and Freya were in the kitchen making supper. Tom's mobile rang. It was Amos, the keeper on the Pentillie estate on the Cornish side of the Tamar.

"Your sheep are about to float off. Their heads are just above the water. They're about to lose their footing. The tide is still rising."

"Bloody things. Thanks, Amos. I'll get down there."

Tom pulled on his boots and shouted to Freya: "Quick, need your help. The rams are in the river and the tide's still rising."

The horizon was a grey blur; fine drizzle fell as they splashed through the mud and puddles on the quad bike. After launching an old rowing boat, which they kept tied up among the reeds, Tom rowed around the sea wall and Freya bailed out the accumulated rainwater. The tide was battling against the floodwaters from upstream. In the murky landscape they made out the heads of the four rams.

"You row now," said Tom, "and I'll haul them aboard."

The little boat rocked and lost ground as they changed positions. Tom leaned out from the boat and tried to heave in the first sheep. It was waterlogged and gasping. As Tom leaned further out the water gushed in over the gunwales.

"There's nothing for it, poppet. I will have to get right in."

He clambered over the side, his feet sinking into river mud, but he was just in his depth, the muddy water flowing around his neck. He grabbed a handful of wet wool and, using all his strength, he manhandled the exhausted sheep up far enough for it to balance half in and half out of the boat. Too tired to struggle, it flopped there like a wet carpet. Tom signalled to Freya to row back to the bank while he allowed himself to be towed behind, clutching the stern. Together they levered the ram onto dry land. It lay in a sodden heap and then, miraculously, got to its feet and shook itself vigorously, sending a torrent of spray over Tom and Freya before wandering off into the gloom. They repeated this three more times. Before returning home, in the gathering darkness they moved the animals into an adjoining field.

Tom had been immersed up to his neck and water ran from his sleeves and squelched out of his boots. His skin was now the same colour as his bluey-grey faded overalls. His teeth chattered audibly and he stood very still. Freya gave him a slight push.

"Come on. Let's get you into a hot bath."

She climbed onto the quad. Tom still stood rooted to the spot. She got off and pushed him onto the seat, shouting at him to help her. Back home and in the bathroom she ran a hot bath and turned to pull off his soaking clothes.

"Come on, Tom. You've got to help me."

Somehow they managed it. Freya peeled off his sodden clothes and helped him into the bath. He lay under the water, not speaking. Freya kept up a conversation while panicking that he was silent. She kept topping up the hot water. After twenty minutes his skin slowly became purple and the greyness lessened. She topped up the bath with more hot water and a tinge of pink at last returned.

After the bath, swathed in towels, they drank mugfuls of tomato soup and finally Tom sank into a bed warmed by hot water bottles. Just before he slept he mumbled, "Good of Amos. Thanks, poppet."

Tom rarely went back to his cottage. Winters passed and now, when he opened the door, it smelled musty, and he heard the scuffle of mice. The wallpaper hung off the walls, and rats had chewed the skirting boards. The furniture, such as it was, was covered in a grey film of mould. Freya had urged him to spend some money on the place and then rent it out. But he wouldn't. He just wanted to keep it as it was, just in case.

As year followed year some of the tasks that had seemed so fascinating to Freya the first time round began to drag; her mind wandered. She often found the winters desperately cold and longed to be sitting in a warm library studying some text or other. Then she would pull herself together and remember that first harvest, or look up from chopping vegetables for yet another stew and see the hedge outside bubbling with birds. But she was aware of a growing tug towards her previous life. She smothered it. She cuddled into Tom's warm body and counted her blessings.

One autumn morning Tom and Freya went together to check the stock as usual. They were both counting and at the same moment turned to each other.

"One missing," they said in unison.

"You go that way and look at the fence and I'll go this way." Tom shouted over his shoulder.

Freya walked along the boundary beside the river. She noticed the rusty stock wire was sagging. Then she saw that the top strand of barbed wire was broken and, further along, the fence was trampled down. She shouted to Tom. He caught up with her and they followed muddy cow hoofprints through the trees and down towards the river. At the edge of a vertical drop the prints turned to long skid marks.

"She must have gone over!" Tom shouted as he climbed with difficulty towards the edge.

"Careful, it's very slippy. Give me your hand. I'll hold the tree in one hand and look over the edge."

Tom peered over.

"She's there. She's down. She may be dead. Tide's on the rise. Come on, let's get down there."

They clambered down with difficulty. The cow was not dead but seemed dazed. No scuffle marks; maybe she had only just fallen.

"I'll try to get her up. Can you get back to the Land Rover and get that rope from the back?"

With Freya pulling on the rope and Tom pushing against her rump with his shoulder, the cow started to struggle and eventually regained her footing. She stood trembling.

"I think she is just shocked. Doesn't seem to have broken anything."

Freya was gently rubbing her back.

"We can't go up. We'll have to take her along the shoreline before the tide rises any further. I'll try leading her and you come behind."

This cow had never been led and Freya thought it very unlikely that Tom's plan would work. But she was wrong. Sensing this was her only hope, the heifer plodded along like a dog at Tom's heels and so to safety. As often happened, Freya was amazed at Tom's affinity with his animals.

Over time the farming world seemed to get increasingly difficult and their lives became more and more of a struggle. Tom never seemed to get the right conditions for sowing, rolling or ploughing. The prices for his finished animals were always falling just when he had them ready. But his biggest battle was with the ancient machinery that was now coming to the end of its working life. Tom, like most farmers, was an excellent mechanic; he needed to be. More and more time was spent in the workshop, where his other skill, as a welder, became essential.

In the front pocket of his Land Rover a dirty envelope was tucked in among old rags, screws, springs, filthy syringes, and all the detritus that any farmer keeps in his vehicle. On this tattered scrap of paper was scribbled the probable calving dates, when the rams had gone in, the calculation for spreading fertiliser and a few telephone numbers, all muddled together but making perfect sense to Tom. The envelope acted as Tom's diary and address book and had worked well for all his farming life. All-important numbers were committed to memory; Freya used to test him and marvel at the reliability of this scheme – nothing to carry and nothing to lose! She was impressed. But Tom now saw that the farmers at the market had mobile telephones. If he passed them on the road, he would see that they had one to their ear. He decided that this was the way to go but found the price exorbitant and changed his mind; the salesman then persuaded him that he could manage with a pager. When he was delayed for lunch, he could page Freya; if she had news about the grain merchant's arrival time, she could leave a message for him. But it did not work quite like that, because in the rolling Devon fields, areas existed where no signal could be found. Within months, the pager, now caked with dirt, was abandoned. Back in the mobile telephone shop, Tom chose the most robust model.

So, the modern world began to creep even into Tom's life, and within no time he became totally dependent on the mobile. It sat, bulkily, in the back pocket of his jeans and, more and more often, it was hoicked out to make calls, many of which were unnecessary.

11

Freya was returning from the little abattoir in Cornwall near Rilla Mill. She had collected the butchered lamb carcasses to take home for boxing up and delivering to their customers. It would be a long night. As she drove out of the valley up the hill, where she knew she would get reception, she switched on the old car radio and heard, "An outbreak of foot and mouth has been confirmed in Heddon-on-the-Wall, in Tyne and Wear." She wondered if this would affect them. Later she remembered thinking how lucky it was that she had already collected the lamb – selfish, she knew – but times were hard and at least they would get the money for those animals. She had no idea how awful things were to become.

Tom had heard the news too. When Freya got home, they just got on with what was in front of them. They weighed up the meat and put each half-lamb in a polystyrene box before setting off into the dark February night to drive around to neighbouring villages, hoping customers would be at home. Freya could never get Tom to ring ahead or plan a journey, an idea that would have been far more economical and time-saving. Sometimes they would find no one at home, but they could not leave the box in case it was eaten by dogs or stolen. She accepted that Tom must do things his way.

On such evenings, they would have a treat and buy fish and chips in the village on their way home. The paper package would sit warmly on Freya's knee, smelling wonderful, but on arrival, she would be too tired to eat.

These were the last deliveries they did for many months. Five days later she and Tom listened to the early news and heard, "All movement of cloven-hoofed animals has been banned."

The Ministry of Agriculture's movement restrictions were severe but seemed to be making little difference to the spread of the disease; during the next week, the cases of foot and mouth seemed to follow the contours of the hills and came ever nearer the farm.

Normally, Tom's ewes, having lambed in the small pens under cover, would first be moved to larger ones with two or three other families and then, once bonded with their lambs, out into one of the small fields next to the sheep houses – there to grow strong enough to withstand fox and badger attacks. Finally, they would go to the far side of the parish and fatten on new spring grass. It was this last step that had now become impossible.

Meanwhile, the majority of the precious South Devon cattle were still munching silage in the sheds. Once they had finished this, they too were supposed to go out onto fresh pasture to calve.

To the north of the parish, five of Tom's pedigree bulls were out-wintering. The holding to the east had good grass and was well-fenced, waiting for the ewes and lambs. If the flock could not be moved there, the chain would be broken and the whole system collapse.

A group of yearling heifers were out-wintering on stubble turnips to the south where the Tamar meets the Tavy. These were the future of the herd. Philip volunteered to be in sole charge of these so, should any of the adjacent holdings be infected, this one wouldn't be and Tom would not have set foot on it. Philip did not seem to mind taking this on; he liked to be useful and never shirked hard work. Each day the electric fence had to be moved, which was difficult on his own, but he never complained. Freya, at least, was very grateful to him. Tom seemed to feel that showing gratitude was a weakness.

12

Tom slept soundly beside Freya. She, on the other hand, lay looking up at the cobwebs with her mind rushing from one blocked alley to another. The cattle's silage was almost used up; the sheep were starving and beginning to break out. Only a third of the way through lambing and they were already exhausted. She slept fitfully. They had come a long way since the desperate passion at the start of their relationship. Now her respect for this man grew daily; he showed such dignity and courage while so much that he loved was being threatened.

Yet another grey day dawned. Leafless branches drummed at the window and rain slid down the glass. Freya's legs ached from endlessly climbing over sheep hurdles from one pen to the other, carrying buckets and sloshing water down her boots. That morning she had a headache and had longed to slump back on the pillows.

They had a quick breakfast.

"Toast, Tom?"

"Just two. Better hurry – I don't like the look of the weather." They drove to the fields on the quad bike, laden with sacks of sheep nuts to fill the troughs. The thin rain on Freya's face woke her properly, and they bumped through the potholes, mud splattering up around them, heading for the flat field by the river. The ewes and lambs started bleating the moment they heard them and came across the field in a rush, desperate for food. The green grass had disappeared and, instead, a sea of mud interspersed with puddles stretched in front of them. Such terrible luck that the disease had come in the wettest spring they could remember.

Lambs born among dry straw and cherished had been taken out to the fields white, healthy and fluffy. Now, they were coated in mud and looked dejected, their heads hanging. They had little energy to keep up with their mothers in the rush for the troughs. Behind the stampede of hungry sheep, Tom and Freya could see small mounds in the mud; that day, they picked up eleven dead lambs. Back in the shed, they examined the cold little corpses. There were lesions and blisters around their mouths and more at the tops of their tiny hooves. Freya knew from Tom's face that he suspected foot and mouth the same as she did. His manner became detached, cool and decisive.

"I have to ring the Ministry." Fumbling as he fished his mobile out of the back pocket of his jeans, he tried to dial the numbers but his hands were shaking so much he could not manage.

"I'll dial it, Tom. You tell me the number." Once through, she handed the telephone back to him. He reported his concern in a voice free from emotion, but Freya could see how much his hands were still shaking as he held the mobile.

The men in white suits from MAFF would be with them in twenty minutes. Freya could not just stay still and wait. She walked off, heading for the sea wall, and stumbled along through the mud, stopping to pick up small soaked lambs, making a pile of bodies. At the end of the field she went through the gate and climbed the bank, walking quickly along the perimeter, swirling grey water on one side, seagulls crying overhead. She was halfway around when the clouds parted and an eerie light shone through, directly onto a nest of Canada goose eggs almost beneath her feet. Perfect and beautifully formed, they lay cushioned in down. They looked quite safe – hope among so much distress.

Across the field Freya saw the men in the white boiler suits and she prayed. Perhaps it would help. As she walked back, she tried to keep the image of the goose eggs in the front of her mind. It was an image she would never forget. As she returned to the sheds it seemed a long walk, her boots heavy with mud.

When she arrived she found the ministry vet and Tom standing over the muddy bodies of the dead lambs lined up on an old table.

The ministry vet now spoke.

"After a thorough investigation I have decided that this is an outbreak of orf, made much worse by the appalling conditions. They're starving too." Tom winced, embarrassed.

"I suggest you ask for a welfare cull. Here is the number." The vet sounded tired and sad. Tom knew he was right and said wearily, "I'll ring today." It felt like a defeat. All those night shifts helping lambs into the world and now this. They stood in the yard as the vet and the ministry officials drove off, the drizzle falling around them and the occasional bleat of sheep calling to their lambs in the distance.

"The cows have all but finished the silage and after that I only have ten acres of fresh grass in all. I'll have to save that for the cattle. So the vet's right; I'll have to cull half the sheep."

He looked exhausted, worn out with worry.

"You know, Freya, I'm going to have to get rid of some of the cows too."

The two of them having had such close connection with the sheep only weeks before as they delivered their lambs, the selection of those to keep was as bad as Freya had feared. They chose their favourites out of the flock. These seemed to be far from the best specimens and more like the lame and the halt; Wildy, a ten-year-old orphan with sun-damaged droopy ears, and Nelson, the Suffolk with a blind eye, were kept from the valley of death. The others, almost half of the flock, were loaded up and slowly the lorry pulled out of the yard and up the hill.

Later that week they stood in the yard watching twenty-eight dear old cows, all in calf, some with udders swollen with milk in readiness for the birth, as they clambered up into the lorry. Some slipped but on they went, clattering up the sloping aluminium ramp. Not one hesitated. Tom had tears in his eyes.

"They trusted me – I've let them down." The ramp went up. Freya saw the odd eye and leg through the air vents. She was reminded of railway trucks and concentration camps. Then they were gone.

A week later Freya drove to Tavistock to buy milk powder for the orphan lambs. Outside the agricultural merchants farmers had to wash their boots in a bath of disinfectant. They did this meticulously; most had changed into clean overalls. Inside, they stood well away from each other and exchanged news across a four-foot space. The girl behind the till was a fount of information and misinformation, enjoying the self-importance of her new-found role. On this occasion, she was full of gloom. She had heard that a case of foot and mouth had been confirmed between Tavistock and Bere Alston. The atmosphere was one of panic. The farmers shifted from one foot to the other looking uneasy, like a herd of disturbed cattle. Freya just wanted to get back to share the news with Tom.

Most farmers were doing all they could to avoid the disease but there were a few who were driven purely by monetary considerations. The government compensation was generous and the temptation to give up, pocket the money, empty the farm and start afresh when it was all over was immense. But by far the greatest number would do all they could to prevent the spread of the disease. For farmers with pedigree herds of dairy and beef cattle with famous lines going back generations, it would not be just a matter of replacing stock. Farmers from the moor had animals hefted to their section of grazing. It was not a question of buying new animals. Their flocks and herds would not know their moorland boundaries and would stray away from home and be lost.

Rumours abounded. A farmer from mid-Devon had been seen dragging an infected carcass across his fields at night. Another had been caught illegally moving animals between holdings.

As she rushed home to give Tom all the news she had to

slow down as a huge lorry, loaded with wooden sleepers for fuelling the pyres of dead animals, rumbled past her. Then Freya came up behind a laden slaughter lorry. The smell of putrid flesh from long-dead carcasses was overpowering; liquid matter dripped from the tailgate. Such negligence made a mockery of the farmers scrubbing their boots.

As she rounded a bend, she found a policeman standing at the entrance to Boundary Farm. The now familiar tape cordoned off the driveway and a large notice said, 'Keep Out' and 'No Entry'. Freya felt fear. She tried not to think of what was going on behind the hedge but she could hear the shots, blunt and deadly.

Back in the sheds, Tom had already heard the news; the local farmers kept closely in touch on their mobiles.

"You do the orphans, Freya. There's one water bag out, the Suffolk in pen three; have a look, it should be twins. I'll finish feeding up."

Later, they got out the Ordnance Survey map and drew a six-hundred-yard circle, using the neighbouring farm as the centre. The line just cut through the field where the five South Devon bulls were grazing. That meant they were 'contiguous'. This new word was now on every farmer's lips; they all knew that it meant alongside or touching. It also meant that all the animals on Tom's holding would be slaughtered as a precaution.

"Couldn't we move them quickly?" Tom gave Freya a disapproving look. No telephone call came from the Ministry that night, so they waited, tense and troubled. The next day passed in much the same way. Tom was short and edgy with her. Halfway through the morning, he threw two bales of hay in the back of the Land Rover.

"I'm off to feed the bulls." Then, picking up a heavy pickaxe handle and throwing it in the back, he jumped in and started the engine. Freya saw a look in his eye that she had never seen before. It made her shudder.

"What's that for?"

"They're not taking my cattle."

"It's no good, Tom." But he was gone, leaving her standing in the yard in despair, the smell of diesel around her, and a fine drizzle falling.

Now they waited nervously for the men in white overalls. Lambing dragged on. They went nowhere and saw only Philip. He was a tonic and brought a touch of lightness to otherwise dismal days. The men from the Ministry never arrived. Had their farm slipped through the net? Just as they began to relax, however, another possible case came under scrutiny over the main road at the farm owned by Albertine Kitto.

A ferocious south-westerly gale was blowing. Up near the road, Tom glanced across to Albertine's barns; they straddled the corner of her four fields. As he watched, a great gust of wind lifted the flimsy corrugated-iron roof. It landed half off, leaving the hay exposed – Albertine's only winter feed.

She had a small flock of Jacob sheep and some single-suckle cows. Passionate about her enterprise, she farmed efficiently and was proud and independent. The previous week the vets had come to inspect a sick cow. The test had come back positive for foot and mouth and she was confined to her farm awaiting the slaughter of her life's work. It was a devastating blow. Tom rang her to tell her this other bit of bad news about her roof. She sounded very old suddenly, a tremor in her voice. Tom's natural kindness cut in quickly and before he realised what he was saying and before he could stop himself, he had offered to mend the roof. A virtual prisoner in her farmhouse, Albertine accepted instantly.

"The Ministry have just arrived – I can hear their car, Tom. They may tell me when the animals are to be shot. I must go. Thank you."

Tom waited until after dark, then, collecting hammer, nails and rope, he set off over the main road towards the barn. By this time he had heard that the Ministry officials had confirmed a positive diagnosis for Albertine's farm and he knew that what he was doing was foolhardy as well as illegal, but he had promised to help, and help he would. He did a proper job and as darkness fell he continued until all was watertight, working by the light of his head torch. Finally back at home, he thoroughly scrubbed all his clothes and boots. But he had given himself and Freya additional causes for concern because of both the illegality and the risk of infection. They didn't tell Philip, knowing he would strongly disapprove. If the main road had not divided the properties, their fields would have been contiguous to this outbreak. They later realised they had only just escaped. Albertine's animals were shot and the carcasses left heaped up in her yard. Putrid oozing slime from the rotting bodies began to flow down the sloping yard towards her back door and seep into her kitchen. She filled sandbags and successfully staunched the flow, but could do nothing about the appalling smell. She was a tough and resilient woman but that awful stench of rotting flesh never seemed to leave her; it seemed to be stuck within her head. Eventually the bodies were removed but only after many desperate telephone calls. She never farmed again.

Slowly, as week followed week, Tom and Freya's fear subsided. Restrictions for moving animals, in place for many months, were eventually lifted, but the scars left on Tom and Freya never healed. She could not drive past certain fields without remembering the acrid smell of burning flesh where a pyre had been lit. A mound in the grass would always take her thoughts back to the piles of carcasses being bulldozed into a limed pit. In later years, if people asked her about the 2001 outbreak of foot and mouth, she could say nothing without a tight pain in her chest as she fought back tears.

Two-thirds of the herd survived. But the whole business had broken something in Tom and, for the first time, he really wondered if the struggle of farming was worth it. His hate for authority grew stronger.

He believed in the conspiracy theory that was making the rounds. Freya listened in horror and sadness as he ranted and raved about the government and how they had purposefully brought the foot and mouth disease to Britain to destroy farming.

Looking back later, Freya realised that this had been a turning point in her relationship with Tom. He hated the interference of authority or anyone else. Tom wanted to live a life free of all constraints.

The continuous sparkle of their love had taken on an ebb and flow and Freya was all too aware of this.

Book Three

1

How many farmers were broken in some way or another by the 2001 outbreak of foot and mouth? Some gave up farming. Some became depressed, some got divorced and some took their own lives. For others, however, it became a clean sheet to work from, and they flourished. Once the restrictions were lifted there were many government schemes to help those who had been adversely affected by the disease and the associated movement ban, not only farmers but also food and tourism businesses.

Freya was aware of these government initiatives and, using her computer, showed Tom the many technical and educational courses for which they were both eligible. These were free, so Tom joined a butchery course; then together they did first aid, and computing skills. It was the latter that really caught Tom's imagination; he was immediately gripped by this technology, new to him. He had an orderly mathematical brain, and within no time had mastered the technical details that took most people many months. He no longer dozed in the evenings; he sat hunched over the keypad, thrilled by the obedience of the machine. It made him feel powerful. He was in charge, whatever the weather, despite the animals, despite everybody else. He loved it and its dispassionate connectivity.

Meanwhile Freya found a vegetarian cookery course in Somerset; her cooking could do with a lift, she felt. It would mean that she would be away for two nights; Tom would have to cook for himself, feed the dogs and the hens. Guiltily she felt the excitement of this small adventure building up. But why the guilt? Tom had managed on his own for years before they met. If she went on the first course offered she could fit it in before shearing.

At lunch one day she broached the subject. There was silence and then Tom looked up. "You cook perfectly well. I don't see the need for it."

"It'll be something new, Tom."

Freya so wanted Tom to share her enthusiasm but that was not going to happen. A small stab of resentment began to grow. I will go, she thought.

When the time came she cooked five meals for the freezer, which Tom could just thaw out, shopped, cleaned out the chickens and tidied the house. Their parting was rather stiff and as Freya drove through the Devon lanes she felt anxious. It was not until she crossed the county boundary that she took a deep breath and began to take in the changing scenery. Fields of bright yellow rape stretched into the distance, interspersed by verdant green fields grazed by black and white cattle. Freya remembered from her school days that the county of Somerset had been hatched in green on the map and dairy had been neatly printed across it. The horizon was intersected by grain silos below a blue cloudless arena of sky. She felt her spirits lift.

*

From the moment she arrived Freya was engrossed in the course. She rather revelled in having her own room with a bed to herself, able to switch on the bedside light and read for as long as she liked, falling asleep with her specs on the end of her nose, propped up by many pillows.

She learned about spelt flour, quinoa and smoked garlic. The ingredients needed for all these recipes would never appear in Bere Alston's shops or even Tavistock's; she'd have to travel to Waitrose in Okehampton. At lunchtime Freya would walk among the rape fields, thankful that she didn't suffer from hay fever. She watched a dairy cow give birth to a bull calf in the field next to the cookery school. Before she left the calf was removed and she knew it would be destroyed: the cow would become a milking machine, its hips like clothes hangers and a huge distended udder giving it a distorted body so unlike Tom's South Devons. Each evening she rang Tom – each time he cut the conversation short and she felt her happiness shrink away.

On the last day they made wonderfully plump vegetarian quiches to take home. Packing hers away, Freya looked forward to Tom's comments; she was sure he would love it. Her route lay through Exeter and she had time to stop at a clothes shop. She felt the usual bubble of excitement and rushed in. There on the first rail was a simple linen dress, mid-blue with the slightest purple tinge. In the changing room she wriggled into it – perfect. She'd wear it home and Tom would be surprised. She longed to see him and felt the familiar elastic pull of attraction.

Driving west, she saw the moor rising to greet her – 'those blue remembered hills' – she loved that Housman poem. She tried to recall the complete poem. Again she felt a slight sadness as she realised she would never be able to share her love of poetry with Tom, and then again the zing of anticipation as the miles shortened between her and home and him.

The door was ajar but no dogs ran out to greet her; it was not the arrival she had imagined. She noticed the wisteria was drooping, washed out and sad and that the bluebells were past their best. The tide was out and as the sun disappeared behind a cloud, the mud looked dark and threatening. Inside, the kitchen was heaped up with dirty dishes and a half-empty bottle of milk stood tepid and coagulated on the crumb-scattered table. Freya called, "Tom, I'm back."

There was no answer and she realised that the quad was gone. He must be in the yard…

She tried the mobile but it was switched off. Guessing Tom must be in one of the barns, she went in search of him.

She found Tom sweating, furious and desperate, with a rope halter in his hand, chasing a cow around the shed. Her arrival was greeted with a grunt. Both cow and farmer had worked themselves up into a frenzy. It was one of his best cows, due to calve in a week, and she was prolapsing.

"Poor old lady," said Freya gently, "we should call the vet." But Tom was in his own world, determined to cope without help, or interference by anybody. Her suggestion was answered with a very firm "No." The cow's distress went from bad to worse, and Freya could barely watch. Trying to help only drew curses from Tom, so she left. Back in the house, for once not exhausted, she noticed the splodge of mud on her new dress and wondered why ever she had bought it and when there would be a suitable opportunity for her to wear it. She then soaked in a big hot bath steaming with delicious bath oil. Smoothing moisturiser on her skin, she tried not to think of the cow and its distress. She knew he should have called the vet. Hours later, filthy and stinking, Tom returned home to his dried-up quiche in the bottom oven.

"How is she?" asked Freya when he eventually came upstairs. She was sitting up in bed with her book on her knees.

"Dead." He tore his filthy clothes off and without washing got into bed. He rolled away from her and snapped off the light.

Freya woke early, but instead of cuddling up to Tom's back for comfort, she lay rigidly on her side of the bed. She felt tense and miserable. Where had the old Tom gone? His wonderful mixture of gentleness and strength that she had so loved seemed now to be obscured by a hardness that crushed her.

At lunch that day neither mentioned the death of the cow. Tom ate his salad, glanced at his watch and then, before leaving, gathered Freya in his arms.

"Have you got twenty minutes to spare, my love?" he said and gently pushed her towards the stairs. That is how any discord was handled. Freya knew it would not do, but there in his arms, the world seemed a very good place.

Ron, the postman, arrived a few mornings later. It was good to see him, as for months all mail had been delivered to a wooden box at the top of the lane in case of contamination from the post van's tyres. During the epidemic, he had missed his cups of tea en route and the brief exchanges of gossip. He wondered if this was like it was for postmen in cities. His enjoyment came from his involvement with the local people. He was forever warning farmers of an escaped bullock or a sheep caught up in the brambles, or he would spread the news of a birth. At least for the farmers the foot and mouth had drawn the community together. That element of jealousy as farmers eyed their neighbours' new tractors or cast critical eyes at the standard of ploughing had subsided, for the moment. Ron and Freya discussed the impending rain clouds racing towards them from the west; she then asked after his baby daughter before he was on his way.

2

Tom decided that he needed another dog to take over from Meg, who was slowing up a bit. Not sure whether she could love another dog as much, Freya was rather against this but Tom was adamant. When Meg next came on heat, they set off to Dartmoor with her in the back of the Land Rover. Tom had chosen a breeder of trials dogs, well known in the area. The dog, Shep, came from a prize-winning strain and the resulting puppies should make good working sheepdogs. There had been puppies in both Tom's and Freya's lives before but somehow these ones would be special. They borrowed a whelping crate and, without bother, Meg produced a magpie collection of six puppies, squirming pink-nosed energetic little things – two dogs and four bitches. Each evening, they would bring them into the kitchen and spend hours deciding which one they should keep.

"It must have a black roof to its mouth," said Tom.

"Why?"

"My father always said that they make the best workers."

"Well, there is only one like that." Freya was opening each small jaw, avoiding the tiny razor-sharp teeth and peering in. "It's the really ugly one."

Freya indicated a squirming, pink-faced, bullet-nosed bitch.

"That's the one then."

Freya did not agree with his choice at all, but there was no changing Tom's mind. Meg was a good mum, but when the puppies were six weeks old, she had had enough. They were rampaging around the garden, tumbling over and play fighting, but at night, they were transformed into silky, sleepy little things who loved to be cuddled. Meg looked thin and dull.

One morning when Tom came in for his mid-morning coffee, he found Freya rather frazzled, the puppies clambering up her legs and chewing the buckles on her boots. Each time they approached their mother she growled and slunk off. Much to Freya's relief, Tom gathered them all up and put them in the back of his Land Rover, leaving Meg in peace. Freya watched as he drove away with six little faces peering through the mesh of the back compartment. It was to be their first day farming!

The ugly one they were keeping slowly turned into a swan. Her pink nose changed to black and her markings seemed to become more uniform, but the roof of her mouth stayed dark. The other pups were quickly sold, leaving Rags, as they named her, to torment her mother, but they became best of friends as Rags settled down. She learned to walk at Freya's heels, sat when told and crept along the ground almost as soon as she could walk; a very good sign in a collie puppy. Freya was careful not to monopolise her, so the puppy spent most days driving around the farm in the back of the Land Rover with Meg. He did admit that Rags showed a lot of promise. Each evening she would walk with Freya around the fields, sit when told, lie down immobile when asked and rush to Freya for praise the moment she heard the command to come to her. Within a year she was invaluable, holding a single ewe in the corner for Tom to catch, splitting the flock for him, rushing ahead to guard an empty gateway. Her energy seemed inexhaustible. Loving and obedient, she stole both their hearts.

3

Freya had an old school friend in Exeter called Jenny. They had met a few times halfway between their homes and gone walking on the moor with their dogs. Out of the blue, Jenny rang one evening to tell Freya that she had made a mistake in her diary and had an important dentist appointment at the same time that, months before, she had booked a session with Daphne, a clairvoyant. As there was a large and non-returnable fee, would Freya like to go instead? It would be a late birthday present. To Freya, this seemed a bit of a waste of time, but she was intrigued enough that she decided to go.

The roads were glistening with sheets of rain and all around gutters were overflowing when she set out for her visit to Daphne. There were so many other things she could be doing but this clairvoyant was famous, and not just in Devon; she'd written several books and appeared often on television. It was a unique opportunity, she reasoned.

She had passed the Somerset county boundary and was now in Dorset. Glancing at the directions, she turned off the main road onto a single-track lane and meandered through saturated countryside, under dripping trees. Her spirits drooped.

She looked again at the map as she approached a T-junction and felt even more uncertain. Just like her life, she thought: one way leads to her career after so much study, the other to Tom, the farm and the animals. She could not have both. Turning now down a narrow steep drive between towering pine trees, she came into a clearing. In front of her was a 1920s bungalow. Freya instantly remembered her Little Grey Rabbit books and thought it looked like Grey Rabbit's house as pictured on the inside cover of each book. Outside, a car was parked, a Volvo.

Pulling up the hood of her mackintosh, Freya ran through the rain to the front door. There was a note stuck to the tarnished brass knocker.

Wait in your car until you see somebody leave.

How curious, thought Freya, and returned to the driving seat to wait. She stared out of the rain-distorted windscreen and shivered. She wished she had brought something to read and impatiently looked at her watch. Fifteen minutes passed. The rain fell more heavily. Then a woman appeared in a headscarf and a Barbour jacket; she hurried through the downpour, jumped into her car and drove off. Freya ran towards the front door, leaping puddles as she went; with no umbrella, her hair darkened in the rain.

A middle-aged woman, dressed in fawn knitted trousers and matching top, opened the door. Not what Freya had expected; rather naively, she had thought more along the lines of black hair, hooped earrings and a swirling brightly coloured skirt! She was ushered straight into a little back room, which doubled as a bedroom. The curtains and carpets were bland shades of beige.

Rather like visiting a dressmaker, thought Freya.

"Would you like to tape the session? Many of my clients do," Daphne said as Freya settled in her chair.

"Yes, please, I've brought a blank tape." Jenny had warned her that this would happen. Freya handed it over and Daphne snapped it into the tape recorder. Daphne did not appear to be scrutinising her and anyway, Freya had been careful to scrub her fingernails well, and remove any telltale bits of straw from her clothing. The sky darkened still more. Freya could hear the rain pounding against the windowpanes. The atmosphere was tense, but Daphne now began to speak in a very calm voice.

"You have come to a T-junction in your life. There are two ways to go. Both will be all right. On the one hand, you have this man; I can see him, animals surround him. He is a little younger than you. He is kind. He is fun. He makes you laugh and you need that after all you have been through. Now I can see water." Daphne's voice changed, becoming sharp and edgy.

"The water is dark, they're drowning." Daphne paused and then continued in a slow calm voice.

"They are in a safe place now, and the three of them are together. The water has gone. This other man, he's still there. He is tall and brown-haired. I can see grey at the temples. As I have said, fun, laughter, you need that. You have not had enough of that. Now I can see another man. He is a professional man. Lots of grey hair. He has water around him, but he is safe. He is on a sailing boat.

"You have this power, Freya. You have a power over animals. You do not recognise it, but you have it. Here you are again, at the T-junction. You have a choice. Both ways are all right. You will have to choose."

The rest was rather general. Something about an older man handing her a rose.

At the end, Daphne asked if she had any questions. Freya looked at her and said pragmatically, "Well, which way do I turn?" Daphne replied that she could not say; it would damage her karma! Well really, Freya thought, this is a very unsatisfactory conclusion.

On the way home, she put the tape in the car's machine. She was glad she had the recording because the whole meeting was now a beige dream. Daphne's voice crackled out of the speaker. Freya listened with amazement.

How could Daphne have known all that? Freya wondered if Jenny had been talking to her? A quick call on the mobile ruled that out.

She wondered about the bit where Daphne had talked of her power over animals. Indeed sometimes, if the cattle were being loaded and were refusing to go up the ramp into the cattlebox, she would say to Tom, "Give them a moment – let them have time to see where they are going."

Tom would lower the alkathene pipe he had been goading them with and listen as Freya talked soothingly to them and they would hesitantly move forward and the tension would be eased and in they would go up into the cattlebox. Meg and Rags seemed to do as she asked them too; maybe this was a power. But she had never acknowledged it as such.

*

That evening, over supper, she relayed the whole experience to Tom.

"Who's this man on a boat, Freya? I'll be watching you next time you are walking along the river." He rose and peered at his reflection in the mirror. "I don't like the bit about 'grey at the temples' either." But he was impressed by Daphne's knowledge and quite accepted the fact that she could see things that others could not.

It was impossible for Freya now to imagine a life beyond Tom, the farm and Devon. She remembered Christopher's occasional black moods and how, if she were patient, he would come out of them. She recognised that Tom had become despairing about farming and she felt the best way to handle this was to be as calm as she could be, to help him and to feed him regularly. Just wait. It will pass, she told herself.

But the clairvoyant had seen something beyond her happiness with Tom. Or had she? It was all a little confusing.

Despite the hard farm work, Freya often took Meg for a walk along the edge of the estuary. Not easy going, as the stones were covered by each high tide and were slippery and muddy. She would wander along, placing her feet carefully, keeping her eyes down to avoid falling. She had often taken the same route when her mother was ill. It made her feel better, and the inevitable ebb and flow of the river calmed her. Halfway along was a little shingle beach where she would pause a moment, sit on the damp stones, unhook her binoculars from around her neck and scan the estuary for birds. The mud flats, exposed by the retreating tide, mirrored the vermillion sunset. Canada geese honked hauntingly and pheasants fluttered noisily to their roosts. Sometimes a lazy heron might rise from the tide's edge and flap off downstream and sandpipers would hop busily about. She would watch diving cormorants and see if she could hold her breath as long as they could while they dived for fish. She would gasp in air long before they surfaced. Often they would take on too big a fish and would struggle trying to swallow it again and again, their heads thrown back. They would scoop more water up in their beaks and try to wash the fish down and eventually they would succeed. Freya would see the lump moving downwards as slowly the fish descended and digestion began; a horrible end. The avocets would appear each October or early November, land on the mud, and without a pause put their beautiful, long, slightly upturned beaks in the water and start to fish in the shallows. When they moved across the mud they would move jerkily like little girls trying on their mother's high heels. She looked out for them each year; it was a marker for her, a time to consider what had been achieved or lost during their absence. Just across the river on this day in early November, she watched them skimming across the top of the waves, twisting and turning in unison. She thought of a quick prayer.

"Please, God, bring Tom back to his old self before the avocets leave."

4

After the foot and mouth epidemic had finally receded Philip left them. To his surprise, on the death of his uncle he had inherited the family farm. Now they saw him rarely. They never became as close again as they had been during the foot and mouth year but on each occasion when he turned up they were very pleased to see him.

It was to Philip that Freya turned on that May day. With a shaking hand and a trembling voice she rang him and hearing her distress he, like a true friend, jumped into his Land Rover and was with her within two hours. He saw her ruined face, tear-stained and swollen, as she opened the door, and he gave her a warm hug.

"It's all right, Freya, I'm here. Tell me what's happened." She was trembling and he gently led her through to the kitchen. Fumbling, she managed to boil a kettle and after tea was brewed they sat side by side. The usual flowers were not on the table and the room looked a mess. Freya was thinner.

"What's up, Freya?"

So Freya told him. She felt he was the only person who would understand. Coming from farming stock himself, Philip knew all about Tom's life and he cared deeply for both of them. Tom was out at a South Devon Cattle Breeders meeting and while they waited for him, Freya and Philip sat in the window on the old tweed chairs and drank their mugs of tea. They had sat like that many times before, during and after the foot and mouth epidemic, but that had been a crisis shared by all three of them. With a prompt from Philip, slowly at first, Freya started to unfold the appalling story just as it had happened. She spoke in a low calm voice.

"I don't know how to tell you this – it sounds so weird. Tom has become more and more in thrall to the computer. He has been staying up late every night. First, it was the making of a software package for farmers so they could tell which was their best cow for breeding. I think he told you a bit about this, Philip. The farmers could sit at their computer, feed in data and come up with the answer. Like you, I tried to be enthusiastic, but I feel as I am sure you do that what farmers are really good at, and love doing, is assessing their herd while standing in the field and remembering each animal, knowing their histories, and figuring out their worth. I suggested this but Tom did not listen – night after night he was up until one in the morning. Well, of course, his farming was bound to suffer.

"During the winter, he became addicted to two television series. It was really odd, not like him. *Last Man Standing* was one of them. Previously, as you know, Tom had never taken any interest in the television, but now he became adamant about watching these two series. In the first, a group of six sportsmen from Britain were flown out to encounter several primitive tribes in distant parts of the globe and trained to do battle with the men of the tribe in whatever challenge they used to prove their prowess. Both teams would battle it out. Well, you know me, Philip. I hate reality television and I hate violence. I heard myself sounding arrogant, telling Tom that I thought it a waste of time and simply cheap entertainment for the masses, and I left the room…but he never missed an episode. He kept harping on about basic physical strength being the true test of a man's worth. Before foot and mouth, I had had an inkling of this attitude but now it seemed to be at the forefront of his mind."

"I can't remember Tom watching television," Philip shook his head in disbelief, "and if he tried to he always just went to sleep!"

"This may sound irrelevant and tedious, Philip, but it really is important. Then another reality TV series came on – this one was about the men of Tanna, an island in the Vanuatu archipelago in the Pacific. The people had turned their backs on the modern world and preferred their traditional way of life. An anthropologist brought four of the tribesmen back to the UK, dressing them up in Western clothes before they flew away from the island. He took them to stay with three different families from different classes. The men experienced life with a working-class family in Birmingham, a Scottish aristocrat in a castle and a farming family in East Anglia. It was only with the farmers that this little group of men from Tanna felt at all comfortable. Well, I just thought the whole thing to be gross exploitation but Tom watched transfixed as one episode followed another. Then he went on about what he had seen to every person he bumped into and I began to feel embarrassed."

Philip agreed. "I started watching that but like you I thought it was absolute rubbish and degrading for the Tanna men."

Freya continued, "I don't know, perhaps I should've tried to talk to Tom and find out what was wrong but you know how it is – there never seemed time and anyway he was so unapproachable. We were always dog tired, just coping with the practicalities of each day. But, Philip, I remembered so well my other Tom – the Tom I so respected. Yes, I knew he was getting further away from me now and that his lightness and sense of humour had disappeared, but I was utterly convinced he would, once again, become the Tom I knew and loved: all I had to do was wait. So I did."

"I'm sure that was the right thing to do," Philip said, settling more comfortably in his chair. "Go on."

"I went to stay with cousins, thinking a break would perhaps help. It didn't. On my arrival back in Plymouth I found that the branch train to Bere Alston was not running due to works on the line. I rang Tom and he very grumpily said he would come and collect me. When he finally arrived, he was seething with fury and said he had not got time to collect me from my holidays."

As Freya was speaking, Rags suddenly appeared at the French window, demanding a welcome. At the same time, Philip heard the scrunch of gravel and the sound of a retreating Land Rover. A slight smell of diesel hung in the air. Philip gave Freya an enquiring look.

"Rags goes off to work with Tom each day but comes back to me at night. We both love her, you see. Shall I go on, Philip, or perhaps you would like your supper before I explain?"

215

"No, no, go on."

"To be honest, Philip, the physical side had been keeping our relationship together and now even that was fading. I was miserable. I felt I was pushing a heavy weight uphill, and forever falling back. One evening Tom scooped up his entire computer gear and shoved it in the Land Rover. I asked, 'Whatever are you doing?' He said, 'I'm moving it to the cottage. I can't work here – too many interruptions'. I felt terribly hurt. Well, you know, Philip, there are plenty of rooms he could have taken over as an office. But once his mind is made up there is no changing it, as you know. So, each day he would come home later and later in the evenings and wouldn't answer his mobile at his cottage, although I knew he had it with him.

"Our relationship was already very tense. Things were pretty bad when, out of the blue, Tom suggested that he should have a 'gap year'. I was shocked, it was so odd – but he'd hardly ever travelled outside the parish, so I thought if that was what he wanted, he should go. It might cheer him up. I immediately offered to do all I could to look after the farm and threw myself into helping him find a project in the Third World where he could use his agricultural skills to help people. Honestly, I spent ages checking the internet for things I thought he'd enjoy. I should have left it to him, I suppose. My efforts only seemed to annoy him."

"Good Lord, how very unlike Tom," Philip said. "Sorry, go on."

"Well, Tom went on about Africa. I had a contact who worked for FAO, you know, the government-run advisory service for agriculture in Africa. I suggested they should meet. Tom was adamant that he didn't want this. I was baffled. Whatever was he going to do? He hated sitting on a beach. He loathed crowds. He didn't like the hurly-burly of travel and he made such a fuss when we had really hot weather. I just could not get to grips with what he did want. He kept ranting on about the unspoiled tribal people, how they had the right ideas, and how we were doomed because we had all become corrupt. We in the developed countries were using up the world's resources. That one I did agree with. Once again Tom's loathing of people in power surfaced strongly, as you saw how it did during foot and mouth. Then he began to talk about Nigeria. By this time, he was not appearing at home for his supper until after ten and he was having lunch in his cottage.

"One night I got desperate. At ten thirty, I drove round to his cottage and left the car fifty yards down the road so he would not hear me approach. I don't know what I thought I was going to achieve. I was just frantic. Before I got to the door, I passed the window. The curtains were not drawn. He was sitting with his back to me, the computer on the table in front of him. I realised he was looking at a dating site, skimming through photographs of near-naked women. Then it struck me that all the women he was looking at were African. I had not set out to spy on him, Philip, but he was just feet away from me and I could clearly see the screen. I was mesmerised. I watched him click from one woman to another, still stopping only at the African ones. I was thunderstruck. The Tom I knew was right-wing and anti-immigration. Well, you've heard him, haven't you, Philip? In fact, he was strident about this – it embarrassed me. By this time my mouth was dry and I was shaking. I stumbled back up the track, utterly distraught. The shock was awful. What had happened to my dear Tom who I loved and trusted?

"I just went home. I waited for him to come back for supper. He was very late, as usual. When he did, I said nothing, but I could not stop shaking. I had been like that once before, when I heard about Christopher and the girls. It was shock. Of course Tom never even noticed." Just telling Philip, Freya felt sick and wobbly. She knew her voice was trembling.

Philip leaned forward and took Freya's shaking hands. "It's all right, Freya. Do you feel you can go on?"

"Yes, I have to tell you. I did absolutely nothing. Can you imagine it? I felt frozen. I could not get the words out. All I did was wait. So unhappy. I felt Tom was unclean. He'd lost his dear, kind, good character. I just went on waiting for him to tell me what was going on. When he did talk it was again about his gap year and his need to get away."

Freya could not stop a great shuddering sigh.

"A few days later, Tom asked me to forward a photograph of himself that he knew was on my computer – it was a very nice one of him – and send it across to him. Why should he need a picture of himself? Then I realised that he needed it to put on the internet for women to study and choose. Was this my Tom?! I felt he was prostituting himself. But still, I said nothing—"

Philip interrupted. "This is extraordinary. Anyway, go on."

"You know how women are usually rather particular about their man's hair? Well, I always cut Tom's myself. It was thick, brown and wavy with only a few grey hairs at the temples. It is a rather personal thing to cut someone's hair. We always laughed a lot and usually ended up in bed!"

Philip raised his eyebrows.

"Well, one day Tom appeared in the kitchen having virtually shaved his head. He looked extremely ordinary, tough and like any other fiftyish bloke you see in the street. I was horrified. When I asked him why, he just said it had been annoying him. I felt as if it was a personal attack. He knew how I liked his hair."

Freya got up and rolled her shoulders.

"Sorry it's been such a long story, Philip. Let's just walk to the hen run and collect the eggs. We'll have an omelette, I expect you are starving."

"OK, but then you must finish. I want to hear the whole story."

Settling down again after lunch, Freya continued.

"A few weeks later I was in the kitchen garden. The sun was shining and the river glinting and dancing in the light. I heard Tom's Land Rover and went to the house with a basket full of vegetables. In the kitchen I washed the mud off the new potatoes and began to scrub them. He came in, stopped inside the open French windows, and pulled off his boots. He was proffering a letter in front of him, like a battering ram. He handed it to me and then left the room. I stood holding the envelope. On it, in his funny left-handed scribble was written, 'A dear John letter!' It was the exclamation mark that seemed so out of place. Inside was a typed sheet of A4 paper. I skimmed over the message and felt a wave of panic. I tore the thing up instantly as though it was contaminated. I still had the knife in my hand. I turned my wrist over and looked at the vulnerable underside with the blue veins running so near the surface. I could not bear a life without Tom. He had written that he would be leaving in a fortnight. The extraordinary thing in the letter – and which seemed to have come from nowhere – was that he said I was too upper class for him. After twelve years? I was incredulous. All that time together with this never having been an issue. He knew my class background the moment I opened my mouth. Within hours, not days, he could have assessed all that. It was not a problem for me. I am sure I have told you before, Philip, his wonderful one liner right at the beginning of our relationship. I told him: We have 'certain cultural difficulties' and he replied: 'You may have. I only have agricultural difficulties.'

"And why was it a fortnight before he left? Why not tomorrow? I put two and two together. He must have been awaiting the arrival of an internet bride. All I could manage was, 'But we are so happy, Tom.' Reaching out a hand, I kept repeating this like a mantra.

"Crushingly he just said, 'You might be but I am not.'

"So now you know the whole thing, Philip. That is what is wrong. Everything."

Frey sat looking miserable and rubbed her hands over her eyes.

"That day or the next I suddenly felt a rush of anger. About time, I expect you are thinking. I collected all his belongings, shoved them into bin sacks and pushed them out of the back door. He gathered them up and threw them into the Land Rover without comment and drove off. So he no longer stays here. But that makes it worse, not better. I still work with him each day. He still uses the dog and stops for coffee or tea."

Philip leaned forward.

"I am so sorry, Freya. Do you think it would help if I tried to talk to him? This sounds so far from the Tom I know."

"I really don't know, Philip. It is impossible to have a proper conversation with him. He is deaf to everything but his own convictions. I feel worn out just telling you about it. I'll tell you the rest another day."

Talking to Philip had helped, she supposed, but her days dragged and her nights were raw and sleepless.

5

From then on Philip rang Freya often just to check she was all right. One day he popped down to see her. Once more they sat in the window.

They settled down, a huge pile of mending next to Freya. Philip sat watching her, knowing that the repetitive act of darning would help her to relax. Freya's eyes felt gritty with lack of sleep but she began again, feeling embarrassed at her self-absorption. Sensing this, Philip reassured her that expressing feelings to one another was part of their friendship and it was fine. Rain slid intermittently down the windows as Freya related more of the story.

"Now, where was I? I didn't tell you about the telephone calls did I? During whatever job we were in the middle of, Tom's mobile would ring again and again. However inconvenient it was, he would wrestle the mobile out of his back pocket, drop whatever he was doing, and move a few yards away and have long conversations. I suppose they were always from Nigeria and not just from his chosen bride but also from other scams. How could Tom, who was an intelligent man, be so taken in by this? He spoke many times a day to some woman called Rosemary.

"'I am in love with her,' he kept telling me.

"How could he be, Philip? So ridiculous."

Philip was a good listener and now Freya told him that she could almost visualise the scene at the Nigerian end.

"'Give us your bank details and open an account so we can put our savings in and you can have half the amount,' or some such nonsense. The group of huge Nigerian men gathered around computers, sweat dripping from their faces, a fan whirring in the middle of a dark back room, all Tom's details up on a board so that whoever was on duty could answer his twice daily emails."

She told Philip that she hated to think of how they must have laughed at this gullible farmer. She tried again and again to tell Tom that Rosemary did not exist – that this was a well-documented scam. He would not listen. He was proud of himself, telling his neighbours of his good luck. Rosemary, of course, asked him to send money for her flight. He did. There were endless delays and then she gave him a flight number and time of arrival at Heathrow. She told him she was thirty-four and looked more Asian than African. He referred to her as 'my Rose'. He was in a fever of anticipation.

"Tom almost carried me along with him, as he sounded so certain, so sure, so utterly smitten by Rose. I could hear myself trying to tell him that Rosemary was not a real person, but it sounded like sour grapes. I could not bear to see him making such a fool of himself but I was powerless to do anything about it.

"One day he explained how he had sung to Rose after practising for hours. He had done his very best and she had been most encouraging but in the background he could hear laughter. Asking who this was, she told him that some neighbours had come in and had also enjoyed the singing. I felt mortified with embarrassment for him as once again I pictured the scammers crowded around the machine laughing incredulously at this ridiculous farmer. 'Tom, it's a scam,' I said but he would not listen.

"He then, at great expense, bought a video camera, packed it up with great care and posted it, registered and special delivery, to Lagos. Rosemary said she never received it and that the postal service was very corrupt. He sent another. Same story."

Philip interrupted. "Bloody hell, Freya. This is terrible."

There was a pause.

"How is the farming going? Just from a cursory glance as I drove here, I thought it seemed to be going downhill – lame sheep, thin cows. Am I right?"

"You can say that again! Tom has just lost interest. He won't concentrate on the farm and doesn't seem to care any more. Although I try to discuss difficulties with him, he seems oblivious to the problems. For instance there is something very wrong with the sheep. Each morning we go out and find at least one dead ewe. I keep pleading with him to let me take one of the carcasses to the vet and on to Starcross Research Centre to find out what the trouble is. He just won't hear of it. He seems to have lost all sense of responsibility and judgement. One day, he was turning a sheep over – he was not doing it kindly – pushing the poor old ewe down. As he did this he said to me, 'I want a subservient woman.'

"'Rosemary' had, of course, delayed and then cancelled her flight as I thought she would and she needed a new ticket because the first one was not transferable to a different day. So Tom had sent more money. He would tell me all these details. Can you believe that? Again Rose had told him when she would be arriving and that she could not wait to meet him. He left the next day in a state of great excitement. Off he went to Heathrow but returned empty-handed."

Mostly Philip was incredulous but he encouraged Freya to continue.

"It is true, Philip. Today Tom seems quite unaware of my desperate sadness. Somehow, and I do not know how, I think I manage not to show my feelings. It is not just that he no longer loves me. He just wants this Rose woman. I am like a computer that has frozen up – sadness and despair all heaped up inside me. I battle through each day, presenting a daytime face that shows, I think, nothing of my pain. I feel much the same paralysis that I had when I lost Christopher and the girls. It is as if I were a page in a book that Tom has just ripped out and carelessly thrown away. I feel abandoned. Oh, Philip, I am so sorry to go on and on."

"Hold on a moment, Freya. Do you think it might be a good idea if I try to talk to him? I have got to come down again next week. I've a meeting in Exeter on Monday afternoon. Would you like me to come to you the day before? Maybe talk to Tom. See what I can make of it?"

"Thank you, Philip, but I don't know if he will talk to you."

Philip arrived late on the Sunday night. The next morning Freya had an early dentist appointment, so after a cup of coffee with him, she rushed off, leaving him to enjoy a lazy breakfast. About ten minutes later, Tom arrived on a quad bike to collect the dog. Philip had always been happy to see him and this feeling instantly bubbled to the surface, so despite Freya's revelations, the two men clasped each other's hands warmly.

"Freya's gone to the dentist. Why don't you come in and have a cup of tea, Tom. I've just made a new pot. I expect there's a piece of toast too."

As he was talking, Philip studied Tom's face. He was wondering if there was a physical cause for Tom's extraordinary behaviour. He looked all right, and seemed totally at home, tucking into his toast and tea.

After the usual exchanges about each other's health Philip said, "Whatever is going on, Tom? First of all, what has happened to make you look for some other woman than Freya? You have been so happy, or so you seemed to be."

"Seemed to be is about right. But things are not as they were at the beginning and I know how wonderful that felt then. I want to feel like that again. You know, I became so sucked into Freya's life. Living in her house. Eating her food. I lost myself. She does not seem to understand that. Her upbringing was so different from mine. I want my own life back."

Tom laughed but without mirth, and said:

"I expect you have heard a lot of nonsense from Freya. She just won't accept that it is over. I've found another woman. She'll be here soon. She's younger, looks stronger and is used to hard work. She wants to be right beside me for the rest of my life. We'll never be parted."

"You had better tell me about it from the beginning."

Philip settled back in his chair with his fresh cup of tea. He sat quietly while Tom talked without a break, hardly pausing to let Philip add a word. Thankfully, Freya was delayed, and by the time she returned, Tom had gone. His parting shot to Philip was, "I need the dog. Ridiculous that Freya has it. Making it soft and useless. Goodbye, Philip. You just need to tell Freya to move on. I am in love with Rosemary and that is that."

On Freya's return, she found Philip washing up in the kitchen.

"Has Tom collected Rags?"

"Yes. He arrived just after you left. Said he was shifting sheep."

"Did he talk to you about us?" Freya's voice sounded sharp and edgy as she walked over to the stove and slid the kettle onto the ring.

"He told me everything as he sees it, and I am sorry that this has happened because like all those around you, I thought you were both so happy."

Once Freya's coffee was brewed they settled down in the window with their mugs in their hands. In Freya's case, the drink was never lifted to her lips. Philip wondered whether telling her would just cause more pain, but agreed when she insisted.

"I will try, Freya, but it is difficult. Tom repeated all the things you have already told me but, of course, from the point of view of someone totally obsessed and in love. He told me about his trip to Heathrow, of how excited he was, and nervous. He had cleaned his rarely used car, filled it up with petrol the night before and driven on icy roads. The journey had been terrible, he said, a blizzard, with sleet hurling at his windscreen. He'd been afraid he'd be late and this would be a bad start to their relationship. Apparently, he'd got a bit confused at the roundabouts when looking for the correct terminal. Finally, he'd found the short-term car park and sprinted to the barrier for the Lagos flight. Rosemary's flight number was nowhere on the board. He waited anyway for the next flight from Nigeria to arrive. No Rosemary. He asked at the information desk and told the agent what had happened. The official said that the circumstances sounded a bit fishy and had given Tom a funny look, which irritated him because here was another person, just like you he said, who did not believe that Rosemary was real." Philip paused.

Freya whispered, "Go on please."

Taking a deep breath, Philip continued, "Tom's words were, 'You know, Philip, all these doubting Thomases are just jealous. I'll show them that she exists, Freya included.'

"Then he said that he had rung the Lagos number and got Rose's mother. Apparently he had spoken to her mother before. She sounded very upset and told him that Rosemary had been arrested at the customs at the airport because she had been carrying a gold bar! This was to be a wedding present for him. 'Dear of her,' were Tom's words.

"Of course I looked incredulous at this, Freya, but Tom just carried on saying, 'I can see what you are thinking, Philip, but I believe everything she says. My Rose is a wonderful girl.'

"Tom was obviously enjoying having my full attention, Freya. He told me all the details. Rosemary had been taken away by the police and locked in a cell. Apparently, her mother gave Tom the number of the guard who Rosemary had persuaded to let her use his mobile. Tom got through to Rose eventually, and she told him that if he sent the bail money by international transfer straight to her mother she would be able to get her released immediately. I can still hardly take this in, Freya. It sounds totally unlikely. He could tell by the look on my face that I could not believe that he could be so naive and be taken in by these lies. But he continued in a rush, saying that once he had made the transfer to pay the bail, he had headed home, and then he heard that she had been released. Although he waited weeks the case never seemed to come to court. He began to get impatient. Eventually the hearing had occurred. Once more he went to the post office to transfer money but this time to Yelverton so none of those prying people in Bere Alston would see him. He then paid the fine so that she could be with him within four weeks. At least there was no custodial sentence.

"Believe me, Freya, I had to really concentrate, because Tom talked fast – he was sort of energised by what he was saying."

Freya nodded her head.

Philip shifted a little in his chair and then continued, "It appears there were more delays. Finally, he got cross and shouted at Rose. She cried and hated his shouting. He'd hung up and didn't contact her for three days. Then she'd sent pictures of herself in a hospital bed, her wrists bandaged. She'd slashed them because she had been so upset by his anger.

"Honestly, Freya, this all sounds utterly unbelievable. What on earth's happened to him?" Philip strode to the window angrily, then continued, "Tom told me he had offered to go out and look after his poor Rose, but she had generously said he should stay at home and look after the new calves. Of course it was 'Dear of her' again!

"I could not get a word in edgeways, Freya. There was no way he was going to listen to my opinion. He just ranted on and on. He could not bear her suffering. He is totally wrapped up in himself. He is going out to Lagos as soon as he can get a flight."

Freya sighed heavily, relieved that Philip had heard everything Tom had had to say.

"Well, at least you understand now how it is."

Swallowing a mouthful of now tepid coffee, Philip hesitated, but then blurted out, "I am so sorry to have to tell you this, Freya, but it might help to understand his side of the whole thing. He felt subsumed by you, your house, your friends, your life. I think you can understand that. I know you were trying to be kind, to help him, but it was all too much. He said to tell you to get out of his life. I've never heard Tom talk like that. Finally, he stood up to go but turned back and looked at me and said, 'Oh and tell Freya to stop going on and on about the dead sheep. I am not going to do anything about them. If they can't look after themselves, they don't deserve to live.'

"I have to say, Freya, he was horrible – sort of possessed and frightening. I can see now why you are unable to talk sense into him – I got nowhere."

The two old friends looked at each other sadly.

"Come on, Freya, let's do something useful. The sun is coming out and we could weed that flowerbed." They wandered out armed with gloves and trowels and spent the next hour doing battle with the encroaching Michaelmas daisies that had formed a Brillo pad of roots under every bed.

Then Philip prepared to leave.

"I can't see any satisfactory conclusion to this. You are going to have to just forget it and forget him."

All he could say to Freya was that the pain would pass and that one day, maybe a few years from now, she would wake up, and it would have gone. A lingering ache, but distant, would always remain as though it had all happened to a different person. Freya knew how Philip had suffered in his own life, and that he really did understand. After giving her a quick hug, Philip then left, bumping down the drive in his ancient but well cared for Land Rover. Freya waved until he was out of sight.

Now she was alone. She instantly felt her spirits droop and with an empty heart went to collect the billowing sheets off the line before the rain came. From the other side of the river she could hear a tractor reversing, pausing, then accelerating forward. She hardly needed to look up to know what it was doing. The Cornish farmer on the opposite bank had also smelled the rain on the wind and felt the moisture in the air. She stopped, the white linen piled up in her arms, and watched as the tractor moved the round bales back and forth, ready to load them onto the trailer. At once, all the pain of the Rosemary months disappeared and she was back thinking only of the past and the Tom she had known, dear, kind and hard-working. That was the trouble: she could not shed the memories, or the love. Maybe she would one day, but it was not this one. Freya balanced the washing basket on her hip and walked sadly and thoughtfully back up to the house. Her tears seemed at last to have run out of moisture and were being replaced by an arid ache.

6

It must have been two weeks later that a very excited Tom called to collect Rags. He jammed on the brakes of the Land Rover. It skidded to a stop. Freya noticed his hands shaking as he undid the back. "I'm off tomorrow – I'm going to Nigeria to find Rosemary. I'll be away for a fortnight."

"But, the sheep, the farm—" Freya started.

"Surely they can all do without me for a couple of weeks," Tom interrupted angrily.

"Oh, Tom, Rosemary does not exist. It's a scam. How can I convince you? Don't go. You're just wasting your money."

"Oh, don't give me that. You're just jealous. Can't bear to see me in love with another woman. I'm off and that's that."

Freya heard herself saying that she would look after the farm; there was no one else. Why should the animals suffer because of this man's stubborn lunacy? Anger would have been the best reaction, but Freya could find none.

Despite Tom's hostility she could not relinquish her protective side. Later, fearful that Tom might be held under duress by the gang running 'Rosemary', Freya persuaded him that if he got into any trouble, he should text her, and in the text include the words 'flat field'. Tom laughed at her. "There won't be any trouble." Freya persisted and eventually he agreed.

In a taxi on his way to the airport Tom called Freya on his mobile. Apparently, he had left an important letter on the dashboard of the Land Rover. Could she post it for him? Then he said, sounding a bit unsure, "Just got this text from Rosemary. She is telling me she'll meet me at the airport. But she is also telling me she's not the girl in the photographs: she's younger and bigger. Well, that's a bit of a shock. But at this stage, I really don't care what she looks like. I'm off anyway. The fare's paid for. Must go."

For Tom, it was lovely to take off from Plymouth early in the morning, see the sun just glinting on his fields. Before the plane pulled away to the east, he could see his sheds and even make out Freya and Rags walking around the sheep.

Not only did Tom see Freya and Rags from the air but Freya saw Tom's plane as it climbed away just above the valley. He really had gone; she shuddered and felt his absence and the emptiness around her.

Still she felt no anger, just total incomprehension and devastation. Perhaps if she could have felt furious it would have helped her. She even harboured some sort of misplaced respect for Tom's ability to just get on a plane and fly off to find this woman in a continent he had never been to. Tom's complete belief in the woman had occasionally almost convinced Freya that 'Rose', whoever she was, actually existed. But then Freya's logical mind would click in, and she knew that this was all a scam.

Freya missed Philip's visits; he had inherited a family farm in Somerset and was no longer a neighbour. She missed Tom, she missed her mother and now, suddenly very strongly, she missed Christopher, Alice and Emma. She felt quite detached from reality – as though she inhabited a different world. Every time Rags heard a distant motor, she tilted her head to one side. She would pause for a moment and then discard the noise; it was not Tom's Land Rover, or his tractor. She'd settle again in a patch of sunshine, just waiting. Freya mirrored Rags' actions but picked up the engine sound much later than the dog.

Freya waited too. Days passed, but it was the nights that haunted her.

7

Freya had promised Tom that she would keep an eye on the sheep. She had finally persuaded him that the cattle should be cared for, at great expense, by a farm labourer from the village. Tom had moaned on about the money. He had now been gone for a week with no word. Then the text messages started. He could not change his travellers' cheques anywhere. Would Freya go over to his cottage and find the receipt for them and text the numbers to him? Freya did this, shuddering at the damp, frowsty smell as she opened the door. More messages came: would she wire out some money to him? She refused. Then the messages became angry. Why had Freya persuaded him to take travellers' cheques? She must have known it would be impossible to change them. She had tried to sabotage his visit. Freya was shocked that such a thought could have got into his head. She tried to forget it. She knew he'd taken £500 in cash and another £500 in the cheques. Why should he need more? She wondered if he was being held under duress. She sent a text that included the words 'flat field', but the reply came back, 'Ha, ha, I am fine. More than fine, having a wonderful time, but need money.'

Desperate now and not knowing what to do, she contacted the Foreign Office and was put through to the Nigeria desk, who gave her the number of the British Commission in Lagos. After several tries, she got through and explained that Tom was somewhere in the city, and that he himself did not know where, and that he was having trouble with his travellers' cheques. The official sounded bored and unsurprised; he had probably had to deal with many of these victims of scams who got themselves into trouble. He did not sound sympathetic but promised Freya that he would ring Tom, find him and sort out his travellers' cheques for him. Eventually, a text came back from Tom, just saying, 'Thanks'.

Freya was acting as his mother, she knew it, but knowing it was not the same as stopping it. She could not bear him to suffer. Despite all that had happened, she wanted to spare him from pain. After the 'Thanks' text, she heard nothing.

Each morning, Freya and Rags would walk carefully and slowly around the flock. Within seven days, the first sheep lambed. Luckily, Freya was on her rounds and noticed the swollen head of a lamb already out, and the Suffolk ewe down and pushing. Rags and Freya caught the sheep in a well-practised pincer movement and quickly Freya felt for the lamb's feet. One was tucked back, making it impossible for the sheep to deliver the large single lamb unaided. She quickly but gently brought the little hoof forward, and with the next contraction the wet, steaming creature was born. Surely Tom would not have left if he knew his sheep were about to lamb? It must be premature, but it did not look it. Freya would have to go round the sheep at least twice a day now, just in case lambing was about to start.

*

In the next three days, twenty lambs were born. Freya sent a text to Tom, telling him. The weather was bad, wet and cold, the worst conditions for lambing. She sent another text to Tom. Should she bring the mothers and babies in? Still no answer. So Freya got hold of dear old Bert who came at once to help. They shifted machinery in the sheep sheds, scraped away the litter from last year's lambing, removed the filthy grey bedding, spread lime on the floor and broke open three big bales of straw for the top layer. They made up little pens around the edge for the twenty ewes and their lambs. With the help of Rags, they got them inside in batches of four, Freya in front of them on the quad bike towing the trailer full of lambs, the ewes following, agitated by the bleats of their offspring, and Bert bringing up the rear. The rest of the flock, presumably due any moment, was housed in another shed. It had electricity, which would make Freya's night checks much easier. They could find no sheep feed, so Bert took the Land Rover into Tavistock and on Freya's account bought a hundred pounds' worth of ewe nuts. It would keep them going until Tom's return. Freya once again sent a text to Tom. There was no reply. She felt worried, mostly for Tom's safety; but surely he would rush home if he knew his sheep were lambing? What had happened to him? She hoped that she and Bert would be able to manage.

Bert's attitude was quite different. How could any sheep farmer push off to Africa, leaving his sheep untended, and at lambing too? It was a disgrace! Ridiculously, Freya found herself defending Tom.

"He must have worked out the dates wrongly, or maybe a ram got in with them early."

Bert only grunted with disapproval.

Bert and Freya worked out a good system that alternated between day and night shifts. Once they had got organised, it became easier; both of them began to enjoy the challenge. There was no time to brood and Freya was so tired that she slept well. Bert forgot his aches and pains and was thankful to be back on the farm and doing some useful work.

After ten days, Freya began to get really worried. She had texted Tom endlessly. No reply. Surely he would never just abandon his farm. She imagined a dark back alley in Lagos, huge Nigerians setting on Tom, and his body lying in the gutter. Once more, she rang the British Commission; the same man answered her call. No, he'd had no reports that a British national had been injured or had died. His voice took on a rather hectoring tone. Tom was an adult and if he wanted to spend more time in the country, there was no reason why he should not.

There seemed no more Freya could do. She'd just have to cope with what was in front of her; she would pay Bert's wages, buy more feed and if Tom did not reappear in another two weeks, she would have to visit his lawyer and find out what she should do about the farm's further running expenses and so on.

Freya crashed the gears as she pulled away from the lights halfway up the Gunnislake hill and the car jerked and stalled. She felt nervous and very unsure as to how she was going to unfold the complicated events that had led her to this appointment with the lawyer. The old-fashioned firm of solicitors had looked after Tom's family for generations. Even the fact that she and Tom were not married would probably be difficult enough for them to accept. She had again tried the Commission but once more they had stonewalled her attempts to locate Tom. The bills for sheep feed were mounting and more straw would be needed soon.

Freya wandered along the Callington high street searching for the lawyers' offices; there was no sign of them, so she asked at the greengrocer's and he pointed up above the shop opposite. There, in large letters and flaky gold and white paint, she saw the nameplate, SLIGHT AND LINNARD. Below it, an inconspicuous black door with a bell. She rang it, and after a few moments a voice crackled from the grille beside her. She was asked her business by an elderly soft Cornish voice. The secretary, thought Freya. Climbing the steep stairs to the first floor offices of the country solicitor, she entered a Dickensian world of gloom; the offices could not have changed for a century or more. A smell of damp old books and unaired rooms, heavy with pipe smoke, hung in the air. Yellowing paint, chipped and dirty, contrasted with the old brown paint on the frames of the windows, long since jammed shut. A middle-aged woman sat behind a desk in the outer office; her red spectacles, encrusted with jewels, caught the light from the single bulb above her. She was the only touch of colour. Ushered into an inner office, Freya shook hands with Mr Linnard. They sat on either side of his big partners' desk, and Freya began to explain the situation. She noticed his tired old eyes wandering over her as he tried to make out what the relationship was between this rather well-dressed woman and his client. As he deliberated, he slowly and carefully rolled up his tie. When it got to the knot at the top, he let go, and it unfurled joyfully down his shirtfront. Freya watched mesmerised and pictured Mr Linnard in his days at Callington School, endlessly repeating these same movements. Now, his old hands were stained to a deep chestnut. She tried to bring herself back to the business of the day.

As she related the story of the farm and Tom and the Nigerians, Mr Linnard's face never changed and his hands endlessly wound up the tie. Freya watched it flutter down, each time exactly the same.

"What about his family?" asked Mr Linnard.

"Tom has only one uncle, but he is no longer in touch with him. He had a son in France but we know nothing about him. There is no will, no instructions, just the usual farm paperwork, both handwritten and on his computer." Freya purposely dropped her shoulders and sat back, trying to relax.

"What do I do? There are the animals, and they must be cared for. There'll be fertiliser needed soon."

"I have a feeling that many years ago Tom lodged a will with us," commented Mr Linnard.

"He may, of course, be perfectly all right, but I have to do something about the stock." Freya wondered if she was being overdramatic. Mr Linnard rose stiffly from his desk, his chair scraping across the linoleum.

"I won't be a moment. Let me look in the back office."

He left Freya in the gloom.

Returning with a heavy lever-arch folder, Mr Linnard looked almost joyful, as if he'd won a game of hide-and-seek.

"Here it is. Now, let's see." Freya fidgeted as he pored over the paperwork. Finally producing a document, he peered at it short-sightedly and said, "He did, but it was done after his mother died. He leaves everything to a cousin, Yves. Did you ever hear him speak of this?"

Freya remembered Tom speaking of his Uncle Albert in pretty derogatory terms. He had been a deserter, stolen a French soldier's identity, then had abandoned his French family, and finally had tried to put pressure on Florence in order to get money out of the family farm. She remembered that there had been a son born to the French woman, Monique. He had been called Yves but Freya realised she had never heard his French surname.

Freya told him that the two sides of the family had lost touch. Five years ago, Tom had received a Christmas card from his cousin Yves in the USA, but no address and no surname. In the note inside was a promise to send on his new details and email soon. He never did, so all contact had been lost.

"Well, I see I am an executor with Yves, so now we have to do our best to find him. I should not really tell you this, but it is an unusual set of circumstances, and one with which I have not had much dealing. You must make sure that what you do does not fall foul of the 'intermeddling' rules. I will let you know, but clearly someone must be allowed to look after the animals. Leave it with me. I will look up the law and hopefully ring you tomorrow. If you can think of the smallest detail to help us find the cousin, that would be very helpful." Mr Linnard leaned back and once again rolled up his tie, unfurling it just as he rose to usher Freya out into the corridor.

Back at home, Freya got out of her tidy clothes and joined Bert in the sheep shed, glad to be freed from what had once been her normal everyday wear. That evening she searched the internet for any mention of Tom's cousin. No luck. For the umpteenth time, she tried Tom's mobile number. Now, there was nothing – no ringtone, just a continuous drone.

She felt sick with panic; Tom and the farm had been her whole life. But she had managed before and she'd manage again. She must persevere, organise things as best she could for the farm, and then get on with her own life. She must just keep a bulkhead between the everyday practicalities and her emotions – she could not cope with both.

The next evening, Freya received a message on her telephone; Mr Linnard had been in touch with the US legal authorities, who had confirmed that Yves had died three years ago in a hospital for the mentally ill.

After a hectic and largely sleepless weekend, Freya at last spoke to Mr Linnard. He sounded less ponderous, almost elated.

"I think you'd better come and see me. Would nine thirty tomorrow be possible?"

Back in Callington, Freya once more sat opposite Mr Linnard.

"I've found a codicil to the will. Young Mr Slight must have put it there while I was on holiday, and forgot to tell me. It was tucked in at the back of the file. It is dated 29 April 2005, so not long ago. It clearly states that in the event of the cousin, Yves, predeceasing you, you are to be the heir. This makes everything much easier. Of course, Tom may come back at any moment, but at least between us we can organise the best route for the farm. In the unlikely event we hear nothing of Tom for seven years, then at that stage we might presume he is dead." He cleared his throat and looked embarrassed. "I'm sorry, my dear, this must be very difficult for you. Until then, possibly with the permission of the court, you can run things as best you can, but not deplete the capital. Maybe you could find a tenant?" Freya pictured the dark alley in Lagos, the blackness of the warm African night and Tom's head in the gutter. She shivered.

"Thank you for all your help, Mr Linnard. I will go back and think what to do next. Perhaps Tom is already on his way home and all this will be a wasted effort." She shook his shiny chestnut hand and left, out through the dusty black door into spring sunshine.

8

Although Freya had enjoyed farming at Tom's side, she had no wish to take on the farm and all the responsibility alone. Every task would remind her of him. How would she ever manage without his knowledge of mechanics, welding, electrics and so much else? The complicated private water system was a mystery that he alone seemed to understand. Freya felt overwhelmed. She went to talk to the land agent, who knew Tom and who ran the livestock market. She had already had some dealings with him; he was now the senior partner, and she decided to ask his advice. He immediately understood and appreciated the urgency of the situation. He had heard the gossip.

"The farm is small by current standards. Do you want to let the entire farm and the cottage?" Freya felt safe with this man in his checked shirt and tweed jacket; he had a solid respectability about him. She sat back and took a deep breath.

"Maybe I am being overdramatic. I think I should wait a month or two. I have Bert to help and I think he would like to work full time. He certainly has lots of experience. I should leave it a little longer. See if I hear anything." She pulled out her mobile and looked at the calendar.

"That takes us to the first of July. May I come back then? Thank you for your patience and your time."

Freya drove home thoughtfully. Once back, and she promised herself it was for the last time, she dialled Tom's number. The ominous continuous empty drone of the mobile greeted her. She snapped the off button and angrily shoved the machine back in her pocket. She would not do that again.

Two weeks passed with Freya working mechanically. Each morning she wrote a long list of jobs that needed doing and she and Bert worked through them. Lambing was now nearly over. Bert spread fertiliser on the fields. The cattle went out, as usual delighted to escape their incarceration. Then the calving started and this year went well, with the dear South Devon cows almost all managing on their own. Luckily no twins and no complicated births – Freya was relieved. Now the lambs were out and chasing each other around the fields. Her confidence grew and with Bert's help she seemed to be coping well.

On the first of July Freya rang the agent.

"We seem to be managing all right. First fat lambs are about to go off. It is as though my confidence has come back. I think I can keep everything going but I'm not sure about the arable side. Could you find a tenant for that land?"

"That should not be difficult," he replied.

It was agreed and Freya ended the call, feeling quite pleased.

Week followed week and the mountain of work gave Freya little time to brood. She had organised the shearing and dipping.

Lame sheep had their feet trimmed and sprayed. She allowed herself just a modicum of satisfaction.

When Freya thought of the red brick wall of her nights of misery, she found that it had crumbled; the urban brickwork was now a softer hue, a gap had opened up, weeds had self-sown, delicate bindweed flowered in the worn crevices. The wall was no longer a thing to fear.

Occasionally she visited Albertine. At first it would be on the pretext of borrowing some purple spray for the sheep as she had run out, but soon she did not need an excuse. Freya loved her company. Albertine's feet seemed so firmly rooted in the ground and she had a calming influence on Freya.

Book Four

1

Freya picked up her binoculars. As she did several times each day, she scanned the river. It was seven o'clock and she had been wakened by the twin blast from the Brittany Ferries' foghorn as it pulled out of its berth in Millbay Dock. So before even sitting up, she had known that there was a southerly airflow coming from the Channel, and that the early-morning mist had not yet lifted.

Now Freya could see a sailing boat rounding the bend near the confluence of the two rivers; it had an old-fashioned outline and was drifting, goose-winged, towards her.

She dressed quickly and wandered out into the garden, the binoculars slung over her shoulder; she felt the damp of the early-morning dew as it crept through her rope-soled espadrilles – boots would have been better. Nearer the river, she studied the approaching boat. A ketch rig, wooden masts, varnished hull, and now she could see the name 'arch Hare', but as the sails were trimmed and it turned slightly to port, Freya saw it was really 'March Hare'; she carried a New Zealand ensign at the stern, and on the crosstrees fluttered a yellow quarantine flag. Could this possibly be the *March Hare's* first landfall in the UK? Freya wondered, for the yellow flag meant it had not yet cleared customs. She clambered down the steep slope to the shingle beach below and gave a wave, which was answered enthusiastically. She was too close now to study the sailor with her binoculars, and anyway, the light was behind him. He dropped the sails to the deck with speedy efficiency and, just as he brought the boat around into the wind, ran forward with a boathook. He swept up the pick-up buoy and secured it through the fairlead to the cleat. The boat rested safely on its mooring and the man shouted across to Freya, "First time I've dropped the sails since I left the Azores."

She watched him lower the Q flag carefully and fold it up. Freya recognised the New Zealand accent and noted the casual confidence of the man. She remembered, too, what it was like to make landfall after weeks at sea. All she had ever wanted then was coffee with fresh milk, a bath and the crunch of lettuce instead of the soft endless mushy tinned food of the voyage. She imagined he must feel the same.

"Do you want a bath?" called Freya across the gap between them. He laughed and shouted back, "My God, I'd kill for a bath!"

He disappeared below and then reappeared with a foot pump to blow up the rubber dinghy.

"I'll collect you in *Sally*," she shouted, indicating the little clinker-built tender on the slipway, all ready to launch.

"That'd be great." He waved, and disappeared below again. Freya slipped easily back into the helpful, trusting way sailors deal with each other. She remembered how it was. She had spent three years before she married delivering boats, sailing back and forth across the Atlantic, having adventures, and now she felt the relief as she remembered the freedom and ease of boat life.

For a moment, she recalled what it was like to be on a voyage; on board a boat with no responsibility except for the vessel. Rowing out effortlessly, she pulled alongside. The man still had the sun behind him; she could see his shape, but his features remained shaded. She shipped the oars and held on to the gunwale while he swung onto the stern thwart of the little dinghy. They were off, drifting gently while Freya fitted the oars into the rowlocks. A couple of pulls and they were back on the slipway, but not before she had studied his hands, which were at her eye level. They were deeply sunburnt, the nails bleached, salt-scrubbed – strong hands used for hauling in sails without an electric winch.

Freya led the way up the bank between flowering gorse bushes, their coconut scent drifting around them, and through the French windows into the kitchen. This was the first time she had had a good look at him. As he stretched out his hand to shake hers, he toppled slightly as though on a pitching deck and, again, Freya recognised the feeling.

"I'm Jack Weld."

"And I am Freya Drummond."

He had a weather-beaten sensitive face, deeply lined, and his blue eyes, behind rimless spectacles, matched his sun-bleached denim jeans. Freya put him at mid-fifties; his face appeared older than his slim, fit body.

She turned to make coffee, asking him about his voyage as she did so. He said just a couple of words. It's not easy, she remembered, to make conversation after a long voyage alone.

"Sit over there, Jack." He sank gratefully into the armchair and took an appreciative long swig of his coffee.

"Wonderful to sit in a comfy chair, and this coffee is nectar." He sighed with contentment, placing the cup carefully on the table.

"Would you mind if I just sat here for a moment, Freya. Suddenly I feel so tired. Must have run out of adrenaline. Do you mind…?"

His words were slurred and already his eyes had closed and his arms fell slackly.

Well, thought Freya, here I am with a sleeping New Zealand sailor in my kitchen and rather a lot to do.

She tiptoed around, clearing up the kitchen, and then went out to post letters. On her return journey, she realised that the petrol gauge was on empty and flashing; she knew her old car well – she had thirty-five miles of fuel left in the tank. Back in the village, she found the garage shut. There was nothing for it but to set off for the pumps at the supermarket, ten miles away. While she was there Freya did some shopping. Some premonition made her buy two fillet steaks. It was well into the afternoon when she returned to find Jack Weld as she had left him, still fast asleep, his neck at an awkward angle. She would have liked to prop his head up with a cushion but decided against it and quietly crept out again.

2

In the years since Tom's departure, she had steered well away from any close contact with men. She was just friendly enough to them but there was a reservation that somehow forbade any form of approach or intimacy. She felt damaged and had no plans ever to allow any other man into her life. It was just too painful. Her heart, she felt, had just worn out before the rest of her body.

Freya was up a ladder outside the open French windows clearing leaves out of the gutter, the sun low in the sky, when Jack slowly uncurled and stretched his long legs. He did not see her at first, up near the eaves. This time, it was Freya who was silhouetted with the light behind her.

"Gracious, is this Jacob's dream? And is that an angel up there?" He laughed. "How rude of me to accept your kindness and promptly go to sleep. Whatever is the time?"

Freya climbed down with her bucket full of leaves.

"Six thirty, and you have been no trouble. I've just carried on with what I had to do."

"It's one thing sailing the oceans, but getting into the English Channel is the hard bit. I've not slept for nights. Just catnaps, so much sea traffic and a lot of fog about. I mustn't get in your way any longer."

Jack slowly uncoiled from the chair and looked down on the *March Hare* as she responded to the swing of the tide and gently changed direction.

Freya hesitated for a second, then asked, "Now, how about that bath, right up to your neck, and a steak for supper?"

There was no hesitation from Jack: "Sounds wonderful. Are you sure you don't mind?"

"There's a towel on the rail," Freya said over her shoulder, "and it will be good to have your company."

As Jack lay back in the huge bath, he looked around and tried to detect signs about Freya's life. No shaving kit near the basin, he was relieved to see, no large slippers, and only one toothbrush. He started to soap his body, loving the feeling of the lather and revelling in the warmth and luxury of hot water. He dipped below the surface and soaped his thick grey hair; it was good to get the salt out of it. In no time, the ardours of the voyage seemed far away. As he rubbed himself dry, he studied a montage of photographs above the towel rail. There was Freya looking just as she did now, smiling into the camera, with what might be two daughters, one on either side of her. But he had seen no signs of children in this riverside hideaway. There was a hazy picture of a green combine with a farmer perched in the driving position, a valley behind him and a river – this river, thought Jack. Then the same girls on skis with a strikingly good-looking man – probably their father; same regular features and endearing smile. As well, there were pictures of brown cows, lambs, dogs and horses; finally a beautiful black and white picture of a London street, flanked by cherry trees. He tried to work it all out.

Back in the kitchen, Jack found Freya involved in an enthusiastic greeting with a very shiny black and white collie. They seemed equally pleased to see each other. Jack stooped to fondle a soft ear and was rewarded by a look of undying love.

"She's called Rags. Usually she comes back filthy but today she looks beautiful, doesn't she? She goes out to work some mornings. She's a marvellous sheepdog and the next-door farmer borrows her when he is moving his animals."

Rags went and lay in a patch of evening sun and closed her eyes, enjoying the warmth and their praise.

Jack was scrubbed clean and his grey hair stood up, unruly and substantial. For a moment, Freya remembered the clairvoyant's words: "lots of grey hair, he has water around him, he's on a sailing boat," and most importantly, she had also said, "he's safe." Daphne had said he was a professional man, so Freya rather tentatively asked Jack what he did when he was not sailing the oceans.

"Well, I still have a half share in a sheep station, but we have an excellent manager so I spend four days a week there, and three practising law in Wellington. It's a good balance."

Freya felt relieved. Was this part of her destiny? But who did he mean by 'we'?

At Freya's request, Jack made them both a whisky and soda. It tasted clean, fresh and fridge-cold.

"Must pick some purple sprouting broccoli." Freya unhooked a basket and led the way to an immaculate fenced garden with raised beds. They gathered a good handful each of the purple shoots and then they moved to the rhubarb inside its terracotta forcing covers. Young pink stalks with pale green fronds were added to the basket.

As the light faded, Freya lit candles. Jack laid the table while she cooked, and then they sat watching the last rays of sun disappear from the valley, seemingly quite comfortable with each other and happy to speak only the odd word.

It was not until they got to the stewed rhubarb with ginger, topped with clotted cream, that they really began to talk.

"Why the Tamar, Jack? If you were so exhausted why not stop in Penzance or Fowey? It would have shortened your journey by a day or two."

Jack pushed back his chair. "Well, this story goes back to 1917. My grandfather's brother came over here to fight in the First World War. Grandfather stayed behind to run the sheep farm – he was the younger – and Joe set off on this troop ship called *Ulimaroa*. They had a whale of a time on the voyage – I've got this letter all about it that he sent home from Plymouth. He had his twenty-first birthday en route, but tragically he was killed in a train accident in a place called Bere Ferrers before he even started his training. According to my grandfather – he's dead now of course – Joe was some chap, clever, a sportsman, and he wrote a bit of poetry. The authorities sent back all his belongings, and among them was this little red leather book. I always have it on board. Full of sparkling poetry. I think it is great. Very rousing, patriotic stuff, a bit like Kipling. My second name is Joseph after him. I wanted to see where he died and maybe find his grave in Plymouth."

"How extraordinary!" Freya exclaimed.

She was sitting forward, alert, hanging on every word. She thought back to her arrival here at Bere Ferrers and how she had stood reading about the wasted lives of those young New Zealanders. She also remembered how Tom had told her about his grandfather and how he had been crossing over the railway bridge just as that accident had happened. She told Jack about this and how the village had been so distressed and that there was a plaque in St Andrew's Church in Bere Ferrers. She would take him to see it.

3

They lingered at the table, finishing a bottle of Merlot. Then, Jack said, "Lovely girls in the photographs. Are they your daughters?" There was a terrible silence. Freya was panic-stricken. She had to say something, so she decided just to tell him what had happened. Somehow she felt he was easy to talk to, partly because she did not know him, and also she thought again about how Daphne had told her he was safe.

If anybody had asked before, she would just say, very bluntly, "They're dead." The person asking the question would look mortified and enquire no further. But answering Jack, once she had started, seemed not so difficult. She got as far as she had when she had told the story to Tom; her relief at having the house to herself, and the work she had to do in their absence. Then she told Jack about her two beautiful daughters. First Alice, who never went anywhere without her sketch book and would draw each member of the family as they watched a television programme. She had just won an art scholarship to Bryanston; Freya's voice swelled with pride. Then, Emma, quiet, gentle, with an overwhelming compassion for all people in trouble and who, even at her young age, was taking a great interest in the war-torn countries of the world; she was destined for an academic future and to be involved in international politics. Their father was fiercely proud of his girls, a very good-looking man, and a hospital doctor. Ironically, he was working on a paper about the physiology of drowning.

They were due to come home from their skiing holiday on the late-night ferry from Belgium. Freya paused for a moment, a catch in her voice.

"Go on, Freya, I want to hear, if you can manage it."

"I wanted to have everything ready for them and to have a peaceful evening, hearing all their news, so I had made their favourite supper, a vegetable curry and treacle tart. It just needed heating up. Emma was already a vegetarian." Finally, in a strangled whisper, she said, "They were on the Herald of Free Enterprise, the Zeebrugge ferry. It sank before it got to the open sea. They were drowned. It was March 1987. That is it. That is where they are. They are all dead."

Freya was shaking from top to toe, her face white. She sat very stiffly upright, holding all her sadness inside.

"Don't be nice to me, please," she stammered. "Why don't you pour me another whisky. Quickly."

"I'm so sorry, Freya. I'm so so sorry." Jack got up to pour the whisky, handed it to her, and then moved his chair a little nearer. "There are no words to say. You poor thing. I should not have asked."

"It's all right, Jack. Somehow I felt I needed to tell someone. It's as though it has all been sealed up inside me. I know I needed to talk about it but there never seemed to be the right person. Sometimes it is easier to talk to someone other than old friends or neighbours." Jack sat in silence, and Freya reached for her glass.

"What did you do? Did you stay in London?" he asked.

Freya told him how she had stripped the house of all that belonged to the girls and their father. With manic energy she had worked all through that day and into the night, rushing from room to room until she collapsed on a heap of old coats that she had piled up on the landing. She had slept there like a dog. When she woke, she had collected all the black rubbish bags and taken them to bins up and down the street and into the next, until all was gone. She checked the house again and discovered a drawer full of old school exercise books and drawings. These too she had crammed into rubbish bags, which she had to take to an even more distant street. She had watched as the early-morning dustbin lorry took her life away. She had swallowed sleeping pills and crawled into her bed and slept until the dawn of the following day. She lost all track of time and saw nobody.

"Then I cleaned everything – scrubbing skirting boards, shampooing carpets, washing curtains. I packed up my own things and that morning went to the estate agent, put the house on the market and rented a tiny, dark basement flat. I crawled into it like a wounded animal and stayed there for a month.

"There were awful things to do. Identification of the bodies, all the contents of the car, endless forms. I can barely remember anything. I wept for weeks and became skin and bone. Then one day, I woke up and it was autumn. I went back to work. I lived for my job and did rather well. I would allow nobody close to me. Later my mother was ill. I came down here to look after her and soon after, she died."

She was sobbing now. Jack rose and lifted her to her feet and, as if guiding a blind person, led her to her bedroom. He plumped up her pillows, and gently sat her down on the edge of the bed. She swung her legs up and lay back. Jack covered her in the eiderdown, removed her shoes, and then sat beside her, gently stroking her arm, quietly saying, "Poor Freya, I'm so, so sorry." Slowly her crying stopped and her breath deepened.

Once he was sure she was fast asleep, he turned off the lamp and crept back to the kitchen. He cleared up their supper things, patted Rags, who was stretched out in front of the Rayburn, and, very quietly, opened the French windows and let himself out into the moonlit night, down the steep path, past the flowering gorse now with its petals closed for the night, and rowed himself back to the *March Hare*.

Next day, Freya was very aware of the *March Hare's* presence below the cottage, but the deck was empty and she reckoned that Jack was sleeping off his exhaustion after his long voyage. She had surprised herself by being so open to a stranger about the tragedy. Maybe it had been easier because she did not know him and he was not connected to any part of her life. She liked the proximity of the *March Hare*, but was also relieved she felt no sense of intrusion. She felt relief that at last she had been able to unburden herself about the tragedy of her lost family. It had all been bottled up for so long – and the Tom story, a more recent agony, just seemed to add to her pain. She pictured waves coming to shore and the bigger one at the back subsuming the one ahead. Strangely, she was not embarrassed by her tears of the previous evening. Jack had made that seem all right. She realised that for years no man had so much as touched her, yet she had not minded his gentle touch on her arm.

Later that day Freya set herself the task of clearing the ground under the apple and cherry trees in the orchard. She became engrossed in her work, carefully saving roots from the wild violets to be replanted further away from the trunks; of course, once the new trees had become established, this would not be necessary. Rags sat beside her enjoying the spring sunshine. After a while a shadow fell across her work and she looked up to see the outline of Jack, with a golden fuzzy halo of sunshine around his silhouette. Rags wandered towards him, her tail wagging.

"She usually barks at everybody," said Freya in surprise. "Have you decided he is a friend, Rags? That really is a seal of approval." She laughed and struggled to her feet.

"If you are not busy, I would like you to dine on the March Hare tonight. She's had a spring clean and is ready for inspection." Jack leaned an arm against one of the original apple trees and tried not to look too anxious while he awaited Freya's reply.

"What a treat! I'd love to."

That evening Freya rowed fast across the gap of water between the *March Hare* and the shore; the tide was running out and she had to pull hard not to lose ground and be swept downstream. That night it was Jack's turn to reveal his skills in the galley. He had made risotto, adding stock and white wine, Parmesan cheese and mushrooms, and to start the meal he had gathered samphire from along the shoreline. This he served heaped on white plates with melted butter and a squeeze of lemon. After their delicious dinner, they both were feeling cosy and relaxed. Jack lit the gimballed oil lamps and the wood-lined cabin became magical, the light bouncing from the polished teak to the brass lanterns, and sparkling on their glasses of malt whisky.

This time, it was Jack who talked of his past. He felt reluctant, wanting to stay very much in the present and savour the moment. Sitting across from Freya, listening to the tide rushing past the hull and the occasional cry from the curlew, this was not a bad place to be. But he took himself back to his home island and the moment was lost. He sat up, clasping the glass tightly, and, in a rush to get it over with, he told her what had happened.

A childless marriage to the daughter of a neighbouring sheep farmer had started quite well, but it lacked passion. It was a good match and he had been swept along by the enthusiasm of both sets of parents. Then they'd tried for thirteen long years to, at least, live peaceably. But the rows had been terrible. Their characters would just not mesh peacefully. There were no children. They blamed that on each other. After five rounds of IVF, and parting with a great deal of money, still nothing had happened. They had destroyed one another, and could find no way even to be just friends. Painfully, they had accepted the fact that they would have to part company. Because of the joint enterprise in the two sheep farms, they had decided on a divorce and lived in different houses but within sight of each other. Jack rushed through the sad story.

"Other people's divorces always sound dull and predictable but for us, for those inside the battle arena, it is unspeakably dreadful. Neither of us could 'move on', as they say. So I decided to take off in my dear old boat. Not the heart-aching story you have told me. Just a divorce. But there is never a 'just' in a divorce. So that is why I am here, I can't face the everyday failure. I have run away."

Jack leaned back and took a long swig of his whisky. And then, looking directly at Freya, he continued, "That is enough of that. I am here, you are across the table from me and you look as happy as I feel. Let's be thankful for this moment. I am only here because I forgot to take the Q flag down after Plymouth and you were there with the offer of a bath!"

They both laughed.

Very slowly, a different kind of romance started to flourish in the valley. Some evenings Jack would row ashore and on other nights Freya would join him on the *March Hare*. They had much to talk about. Jack told her of his life on the sheep farm, of riding in the outback early in the morning, of campfires and southern skies, and Freya slowly unravelled the story of Tom, until there were no more secrets between them.

There may not have been secrets, but Freya had a long way to go before she could relinquish her hard-won independence and recover from her loss. There was never any word from Tom, but in Freya's heart she felt she would never again find that which she had had with him. There had been a sort of equality in the depth of their passion for one another. Freya sometimes looked in her desk for pens and pencils and there, tucked in a cubbyhole, she would sometimes find a cheque on which she had written the amount 'all my love' and attached to it a receipt from Tom, 'total balance'. It was childish, she knew, but that was how it had seemed. She had to pull herself together. Perhaps life would never be like that again, but it might just be different. Another kind of love.

Jack pulled himself up through the hatch, rested his elbows on the coach-house roof and looked downstream. It could have been North Island. He felt a sudden wave of homesickness but, turning towards the bank, a splash of colour among the greenery caught his eye. There she was in a bright red sarong, a bucket in one hand, heading for the chicken coop. Freya was the cause of his happiness but also the reason for his thoughtfulness, and he knew that they were going to have to say something and to decide one way or another. He was feeling wonderfully alive and truly happy but, after a while, a sort of vacuum had settled around them, a feeling of tension. He had finished his writing, revised it twice, sent it off and there was no longer any excuse to linger on the Tamar – except for the woman up there, the one feeding the hens.

Just as Freya was heading towards the hen coop she glanced, as usual, down to where the *March Hare* was swinging on her mooring. Had she grown so fond of Jack that she would leave her beloved valley and start a new life in New Zealand? She knew he felt he should head back to the sheep station. She knew that part of him did not want to go. They seemed to be stuck in a bit of a muddle – both too mature just to jump into a new life. After Tom, who she had so totally trusted and loved, could she feel safe ever again? Or was she really happy to live her life out without comradeship, without sharing, alone in this beautiful place? Was it enough?

4

On 27 September, both Freya and Jack stood with heads bowed at the short service in memory of the New Zealand soldiers. It was held on the railway platform and the vicar had asked Jack to lay a wreath on the disused train track where the tragedy had occurred. Freya liked the feeling of pride she felt as she watched Jack, tall, straight-backed and handsome as he walked forward. He had on a reefer jacket, which he had hung up overnight to get rid of any creases, and a blue shirt to match his remarkable dark-cobalt eyes. He had stood there in front of the small gathering, the wind ruffling his grey hair, and read one of his Uncle Joe's poems. There had been a catch in his voice, and for a moment all was quiet, each person wrapped in his or her own thoughts. Then the little group of people, led by the vicar, had walked down the hill to the church, chatting quietly together, no one wanting to be jolted away from this solemn moment. As they passed the war memorial and on through the lynch gate, they could see the River Tavy just beyond the gravestones. Once in the church, they gathered in front of a curtained plaque, which was to be unveiled by the New Zealand High Commissioner. Freya thought of the mothers back in New Zealand and how futile the deaths of their sons must have felt.

Then she thought of Christopher, Alice and Emma and, to her immense shame, she felt a sob rising and quickly reached for Jack's pocket and his large, clean white handkerchief. She felt his arm around her shoulders; she pulled herself together and, for a moment, allowed herself to be looked after.

Tea was laid on for them in the village hall, so they wandered back through the graveyard. Jack and Freya looked idly at the lichen-encrusted ancient tombstones. At Tom's parents' stone, Freya stopped. There was Florence's name below William's; somehow Freya felt a great bond with this woman. She remembered a brief conversation with Bert when they had been going through the flock to check for fly strike. Freya had been pushing the sheep along the race with the help of Rags, and Bert had been giving them a good look over and then drenching them with wormer. They had stopped to have tea from Freya's flask, and in that brief moment, perched on some straw bales, Bert had told her about Florence. She was a legend in the village, a beautiful young girl. Every man in the parish had been besotted by her. During the war, she had met this New Zealander. He was called Frank Weld and she had fallen in love with him. She only had eyes for Frank. She was on her honeymoon when he'd gone off as part of the D-Day landings. He had died before he reached the French beach. Bert had sounded angry and said, "They'd been dropped into too deep water. Bloody awful mistake from the officer in charge. Whole landing craft full of young blokes. All dead. All drowned."

Then he told her how Florence, heartbroken, had left the area, unable to face anybody or any place that reminded her of her dead husband. Two years passed; she lived and worked in

Exeter but at weekends would return to visit Edna and Walter. Each time she returned to the parish she had seen William and slowly he had wooed her.

"I knew him then. He took his time and in the end he got what he wanted and their marriage was more than successful. We all envied William. Florence was a beauty, inside and out. He was a good husband to her, mind, but it was a more peaceful sort of thing." Bert had looked thoughtful. Something about the memory of that conversation made Freya want to talk to Bert and hear the story again.

While Freya and Jack took their time beside the family gravestone, Jack had stooped to look closely at a brass plaque half hidden in the grass.

"Look, Freya." He was bending back the tussocks to read the inscription.

"It says, 'In memory of Frank Weld from Wellington, North Island, New Zealand Lost 6 June 1944. Much loved.'"

Freya dropped down beside Jack and read it for herself.

"It was a generous act of William's to put the memorial next to his own family tombstone. He knew that one day Florence would be buried there too. What a nice man."

After the ceremony and the tea at the village hall most of the gathering had moved towards the pub. Freya used to visit the Old Plough with Tom but had not been since his departure to Nigeria. She felt as though all eyes were upon her and she wished they could think of her as a complete person, not just an adjunct to Tom. In the pub, Jack quickly got involved in a complicated discussion with a neighbouring farmer about the different techniques of shearing, and Freya was pleased to see Bert in the corner, beckoning her over. She joined him. Jack brought two glasses of cider across for them and then returned to his discussion on the finer points of the Bowen technique, a complicated procedure quite unlike how they sheared sheep in Devon.

"Can you remind me, Bert, about Florence and her first husband?" Freya asked.

"It was a sad old thing. Florence had loved him so passionately and grieved for a brave while. But it seemed that her love for William was different. Neither better nor worse, just different." Then Bert looked Freya very straight in the eye.

"I know how much you have suffered, maid. You had something really special with Tom. But there are different kinds of love. Don't let all that hurt hide a good thing from your eyes." He nodded towards Jack.

"That's a good bloke, maid. You have waited long enough for that lunatic to come home, and would you want him if he did? You were blinded by love or lust or some such thing. Time to move on." Freya had never heard Bert make such a long and thoughtful speech.

"Bert, I have no one to advise me. I'm just frightened. Frozen like a rabbit in the headlights. I appreciate your wise old words. I'm not waiting for Tom. I'm just being a wimp. Too fearful of failure and all the pain it can bring. I have battled to put myself in a safe place. I do not want to be vulnerable again. But I expect you are right. Thank you, Bert." Freya gave him a wave and returned to find Jack demonstrating how to hold a sheep the New Zealand way, using the long-suffering Rags to demonstrate. She was upside down on the floor, much to the amusement of the farmers who had gathered around. Rags, however, was not impressed as she had been in the middle of a game with the pub dog!

Back at home, Freya thought long and hard about Bert's uncharacteristically philosophical words. Maybe the sexual excitement of her relationship with Tom had blinded her to all his faults. She had endlessly made excuses for his farming mistakes, had turned a blind eye to his bull-headed obstinacy, calling it strength when it had really been ignorance. He had, she realised, never been able to take personal responsibility for anything. He had always blamed the government, the weather, or her. Now, when she thought about it, she realised he had been totally self-centred, never considering anyone's needs but his own. Thinking back over those years, she had given Tom the benefit of the doubt, and had decided that his increasingly negative attitude was a passing depression that would right itself if she just waited. But it had not. Freya pulled her mind away from thinking of all those years in which she had devoted so much time and energy to Tom and his farming. And all for what? What a waste. Instead, she tried to concentrate on the good times they had had: she had learned so much about farming; they had laughed and loved in the sunshine and had been happy for much of that time. From now on, she would try to look at it that way; any other way was self-destructive.

5

Once, as Jack and Freya were driving out of the village, Jack had asked her about the field of solar panels on their right. They looked out of place in this rural parish, lined up like a military graveyard. Freya told him the story of the field Tom had sold off to raise some capital for new machinery. He had then rented it back from the mystery owner. Within five years, a planning application had gone in to the local council for the erection of solar panels. Tom had been given notice to terminate his tenancy. The payback tariff had been large in those days and Tom had worked out the figures and been furious at how much money he could have made for himself if he had not sold the field. Freya had known that he would never have been far-sighted enough to invest in solar power. But he had been bitter about it. He had strongly objected to the planning application but had been overruled. He had stored the experience away, one more scar. Freya fell silent after telling this story, feeling almost guilty for showing the sour side of Tom's character.

Jack had become first of all Freya's friend, and it was only with his gentle presence that she realised how lonely she had been. It made all the little things seem worthwhile and halved the difficulties. With Jack, there was music to listen to, books to share; they had sailed together, played tennis, battled it out on the chessboard, enjoyed solving the crossword after dinner. He was a true companion. She had not experienced this with either Christopher or Tom. Christopher was always working hard to move up the medical ladder and was usually at the hospital late into the night. Freya was pretty sure by now that she wanted Jack beside her for ever but she had been just too frightened of getting hurt, of exposing herself again. Now Bert's words gave her the push she needed.

Freya and Jack had walked along the path deep into the woods parallel with the river, a path that had been used by the miners. When the mines had closed, the whole slope had been cleared with dynamite to turn the steep south-facing ground into horticultural holdings known as 'gardens'.

"Look." Freya pointed. At their feet, among the leaves, she had found sweet chestnuts.

"We must gather them before the squirrels get them."

But Jack was lost in a dream of long ago, still focused on Freya's previous words. She had spoken of the short-legged old man towing the tin bath step by step up the precipitous slope. Jack imagined him and his struggle, driving one foot in front of the other; the bath filled with earth that had run down to the bottom of the hill, leaving the hard-won cultivation devoid of topsoil. At night, after his day's work, the man would harness himself up, defying gravity, and tow the precious fertile soil back to the top of the slope.

The path was soft beneath them, carpeted by many layers